The View from Here

NIMROD INTERNATIONAL JOURNAL

The View from Here

Nimrod International Journal is indexed in
HUMANITIES INTERNATIONAL COMPLETE

ISBN: 0-9794967-9-9   ISSN: 0029-053X
Volume 55, Number 2
Spring/Summer 2012

THE UNIVERSITY OF TULSA — TULSA, OKLAHOMA

The University of Tulsa is an equal opportunity/affirmative action institution. For EEO/AA information, contact the Office of Legal Compliance at (918) 631-2602; for disability accommodations, contact Dr. Jane Corso at (918) 631-2315.

*This issue of Nimrod is dedicated to
Dr. George Hamley Odell,
1942-2011*

*Professor of anthropology,
internationally recognized archaeologist,
loved by his students and friends,
and always a jaunty sight
with Frieda by his side*

Editorial Board

Editor-in-Chief	Francine Ringold
Managing Editor	Eilis O'Neal
Associate Editor	Diane Burton
Poetry Editors	Lisa Ransom, Ann Stone
Associates	Patricia Addis, Sara Beam, Don Buthod, Ivy Dempsey, William Epperson, Britton Gildersleeve, Sue Gronberg, Cynthia Gustavson, Grant Jenkins, Mary McAnally, Caleb Puckett, Bruce Tibbetts, Frances Tibbetts
Fiction Editor	Susan Mase
Associates	Colleen Boucher, Mary Cantrell, Henry Cribbs, Sloan Davis, Emily Dial-Driver, Kim Doenges, Ellen Hartman, Carol Johnson, Mary Larson, Andrew Marshall, Geraldine McLoud, Jim Millaway, Claudia Nogueira, Joshua Parrish, Harry Potter, Diane Seebass, A. J. Tierney, Krista Waldron
Editorial Assistants	Shelli Castor, Samantha Jones, Helen Patterson, Dmitry Yevtushenko
Production Manager	Susan Coman, Protype, Tulsa, OK
Editorial Consultants	S. E. Hinton, Yevgeny Yevtushenko, Tulsa, OK; Linda Bierds, Seattle, WA; Ronald Christ, Santa Fe, NM; Sydney Janet Kaplan, University of Washington; Joseph Langland, Emeritus Professor, Amherst University; Margot Norris, University of California at Irvine
Front and Back Cover Art	Leslie Ringold, photographs
Cover Design	Susan Coman, Protype, Tulsa, OK

Advisory Board

Caroline Abbott, Attorney; Ellen Adelson, Clinical Social Worker; Adrian Alexander, Dean of McFarlin Library, TU; Mark Barcus, Special Judge for Tulsa County; Dale Thomas Benediktson, Dean, Arts & Sciences, TU; Harvey Blumenthal, Neurologist; Marvin Branham, Public Relations; Gary Brooks, Allomet Partners, Ltd.; Nona Charleston, Director of Nationally Competitive Scholarships, TU; John Coward, Professor of Communications, TU; Katherine Coyle, Attorney; Stephani Franklin, Architectural Landscape Designer; Charles Hatfield, Professor of Literature, University of Texas at Dallas; Evelyn Hatfield, Consultant; Bill Hermann, Chemical Engineer; Doug Inhofe, Attorney; Sam Joyner, former U. S. Magistrate Judge (Chair); Hilary Kitz, Political Consultant; Sandra Langenkamp, Consultant; Maria Lyda, Educational Consultant; Jeff Martin, Distribution Consultant; Robert Mase, Oil and Gas Producer; John Novack, Architect; Donna O'Rourke, Advertising Consultant; Joan Seay, Editor; Robert Spoo, Professor of Law, TU; Gordon Taylor, Professor of English, TU; Tom Twomey, Media Consultant; Jackie van Fleet, Literary Consultant; Melissa Weiss, Psychiatric Social Worker; Joy Whitman, Systems Manager; Fred Wightman, Educator; Randi Wightman, Art Consultant; Penny Williams, Former State Senator; Jane Wiseman, Civil Appeals Judge; Rachel Zebrowski, Architect

Acknowledgements

This issue of *Nimrod* is funded by donations, subscriptions, and sales. *Nimrod* and The University of Tulsa acknowledge with gratitude the many individuals and organizations that support *Nimrod*'s publication, annual prize, and outreach programs: *Nimrod*'s Advisory and Editorial Boards; and *Nimrod*'s Angels, Benefactors, Donors, and Patrons.

ANGEL ($1,000+) — Ellen and Steve Adelson, Margery Bird, Joan Flint, Stephani Franklin, George Krumme, Susan and Robert Mase, Harry Potter, Randi and Fred Wightman, The John Steele Zink Foundation

BENEFACTOR ($500+) — Adrian Alexander, Ivy and Joseph Dempsey, The Jean and Judith Pape Adams Foundation, Cynthia Gustavson, Ruth K. Nelson, Donna O'Rourke and Tom Twomey, Lisa Ransom and David Flesher, Ann Daniel Stone, The Kathleen Patton Westby Foundation, Joy Whitman, Jane Wiseman

DONOR ($100+) — Ann Bartlett, Harvey Blumenthal, Diane Burton, Kenneth Bruce, Mary Cantrell and Jason Brimer, Barbara Bucholtz, Katherine and John Coyle, Harry Cramton, Kimberly Doenges, Kay and Daniel Duffy, Marion and William Elson, Nancy and Ray Feldman, Ken Fergeson, Sherri Goodall, Helen Jo Hardwick, Ellen Hartman, Nancy and William Hermann, Robert James, Elizabeth and Sam Joyner, The Kerr Foundation, Marjorie and David Kroll, Lydia Kronfeld, Robert LaFortune, Steve Liggett, Roberta Marder, Rita Newman, Catherine Gammie Nielsen, Brent Pallas, Nancy and Thomas Payne, Pamela Pearce, Judy and Rodger Randle, Carol Redford, Patricia Rohleder, Andrea Schlanger, Diane Seebass, Glenda and Larry Silvey, Gene Starr, Fran and Bruce Tibbetts, Dian Trompler, Marlene and John Wetzel, Melissa and Mark Weiss, Michelle and Clark Wiens, Josephine Winter, Mary Young and Joseph Gierek, Linda Young, Rachel Zebrowski, Ann Zoller

PATRON ($50+) — Rouslana Andriyonova, Helen and M. E. Arnold, Rilla Askew, Margaret Audrain, Sue and William Flynn, Marilyn Inhofe, Lynda Jacobs, Carol Johnson, Simon Levit, Olivia Marino, Chris Matthies, Geraldine McLoud, Connie Murray, Lynne and John Novack, Joan Seay, Carolyn Taylor, Renata and Sven Treitel, Stephanie De Verges, Krista and John Waldron, Ann Watson, Ruth Weston, Martin Wing

Table of Contents

Francine Ringold	xi	Editor's Note

Prose

Catherine Browder	25	Departures
Ihab Hassan	61	Tahrir
LaTanya McQueen	85	On the Terra Roxa Earth We Saw . . .
Vince Sgambati	135	Grave Companions
Stephanie Dickinson	179	JadeDragon_77

Poetry

Robin Chapman	1	Hubble Maps Dark Matter
	2	April 1: Madison
Karina Borowicz	3	Edges
Eric Pankey	4	Essay on Idleness
	5	June Depression
Eleanor Paynter	6	Dismantling the Hive
	7	Cow Tipping
	8	Into Illinois
Margaret Rozga	9	Eden
	10	Recall
Myra Shapiro	11	I am a Tree. Look at Me.
Travis Mossotti	12	The Story of a Plant
Julianna McCarthy	13	In the Bedroom
	14	There Should Have Been Flowers
Daniel Lusk	15	A Room in the Woods
	17	When Horses Love
	19	How the Story Begins: Prelude to . . .
Grace Cavalieri	22	Vanished Reflections
Rick Bursky	23	The Nature of the Correspondence . . .
	24	Ex Cathedra
Jonathan Greenhause	44	Departing from *Sengen Jinja*
	45	Honeymoon
Tomaž Šalamun	46	They All
	47	Poppy
	48	Full Moon
Patricia Fargnoli	49	Biography from Seventy-Four
Bryce Lillmars	51	Borgo's
Matt Schumacher	53	The World's Only Wooden Skyscaper
John A. Nieves	54	A Few Personal Notes on the Recipe . . .
Gail Peck	55	Postcard of Provence

Andrew Grace	56	Hay
Kitty Jospé	58	Postcards
	60	Overheard in my Neighborhood
James K. Zimmerman	73	The Dream About the Plane
William Winfield Wright	74	The View from Space
	75	Close to the Water
Emily Benson	76	The Problem with Paradise
	77	The Day's Catch
Stan Zumbiel	78	Eddie Autumn and His Trio
Suze Baron	82	Lucienne
Nadine Sabra Meyer	83	The Lace-Maker's Bloom
Jose Trejo-Maya	84	Chilam Balam
Darrel Alejandro Holnes	97	Pagan
Edward Adams	99	Conspiracy
Jane Vincent Taylor	100	On the Train, Traveling . . .
Martin Ott	101	Cloud Writing
	102	Fruits of Labors
Linda Pastan	103	Choosing Sides
Thomas Patterson	104	Room With a View, 1944
Sally Allen McNall	105	Onset
Benjamin Myers	106	Agincourt
Amy Vaniotis	107	Fallen Marine
Lee Rossi	108	A Field
	110	A Tour of Scotland . . .
Jamie Ross	111	Day Tripper
Rebecca Lehmann	112	Its Likeness Is the World
Jim Daniels	113	Ducking
	115	Charity's Anonymous . . .
Lisa D. Schmidt	117	Squirrel in the Attic
Francine Marie Tolf	118	Sky
Barbara Swift Brauer	119	Toward Winter
	120	Missing Her
Jeff Gundy	121	Subjunctive on Burntside . . .
Marita Garin	122	Nostalgia
Clark Smith	124	The Bald Guy
Dian Duchin Reed	126	Out of Sight
Kathleen Kirk	127	Before I Can See
	128	A window shalt thou make
Molly Tenenbaum	129	During the Night . . .
Laurelyn Whitt	131	Holding On

ix

Geri Rosenzweig	132	From Night's Libretto
	133	I Want to Wake up Again
Ines P. Rivera Prosdocimi	134	Love Letter to an Afterlife
Rachel Inez Lane	145	Dyslexia is a Lonely Cloud
Becky Kennedy	148	Returning
T. Alan Broughton	149	Doorways
	150	Tree House
Victoria Kelly	151	To My Husband . . .
LeRoy N. Sorenson	152	Ghosts at Craigville
Denise Bergman	153	Alaska: Turnagain Bay
Marge Piercy	155	Tsunami
	156	All fall down
Angela Patten	157	The Weather in Toronto . . .
Jefferson Harris	158	The Elephant Seals
Penelope Scambly Schott	159	The Cliffs Beyond Akaroa
Brad Johnson	160	The Birds
Susan Cohen	161	Lucky Dog
Monica Wendel	162	"Wikileaks Reveals That . . ."
Dwayne Thorpe	163	Noon Whistle
Tara Taylor	164	Something Else
Christine Hope Starr	166	Handloom Fabrics
John Surowiecki	167	D.D. (Elegy for a Copywriter)
	168	A.B. (Four Last Songs)
	170	Making My Sister Laugh
Simon Perchik	171	*
Christopher Robinson	172	Cicatrix
E. Louise Beach	173	Ombra mai fù
	174	Vocalise
Mekeel McBride	175	Gazebo
	176	What If
Ann Hostetler	177	Enough
	178	Flight Patterns
Kathryn Nuernberger	196	*The Symbolical Head* (1883) . . .
	197	Or Perhaps Not
	198	René Descartes and the . . .
Ed Frankel	200	Among Other Things, . . .
About the Authors	203	
About the Artists	215	

Francine Ringold

Editor's Note

Every year, for *Nimrod*'s spring issue, we select a theme; this year, after a good deal of thought, our theme is "The View from Here." As so often, the theme is both a creation and a discovery. Already on hand, carefully saved and edited, from the thousands of manuscripts we receive each year we had selections that seemed to fit under that rubric. Then we announced the forthcoming theme to give other writers an opportunity to share their perspectives, their poems and stories and essays, some already written, awaiting just the right invitation to submit for publication, some inspired by our announced theme. The manuscripts tumbled in, by the hundreds—earnest, playful, passionate, precise.

Selection from such wealth is a challenge. And then, what order do we construct to best illuminate the many inventive ways our authors found to sight from here and here and here . . . from a wheelchair, from the top of skyscraper, focused by a Hubble telescope or a pinhole camera? Is there a distinctive outlook in spring or winter? Does the look change departing Sengen Jinja, Russia, Slovenia, Scotland? Of course. And overriding each perspective is the concern with not just what is said, but, as John Ciardi admonished, how we say what we say. It is a dizzying task to read, select, and order this kaleidoscopic vision and we have relished it.

The issue begins with Robin Chapman's view from the Hubble's eye in "Hubble Maps Dark Matter," slant and internal rime bending the form, "teaching us how to see what we cannot see." And suddenly, spring overturns the earth. No longer looking up to the heavens, bees are everywhere, we can even "hear a mouse's heartbeat" in Chapman's "April 1: Madison," especially if we become the thing we are observing, as from within Myra Shapiro's "I am a Tree. Look at Me." And especially if we are patient, "wait in the tunnel of the moon's eclipse" as "night's small things" become visible, as they do for Julianna McCarthy. Later in the issue it is winter that writes its blizzards, clouds, and slowed steps across the sky—a different vision of the tricks light plays.

Inspiration is also to be found in looking hard and clear through a window, framed by a door, from Daniel Lusk's "A Room in the Woods." Both he and Grace Cavalieri build their poems from a mere glimpse of a girl who steps out of the trees; Rick

xi

Bursky sees every letter of the alphabet as having once been a "soldier . . . marching through a muddy field," for writing, like life, is an act of courage.

Nor are the views of war in this issue only metaphorical: Thomas Patterson's "Room With a View, 1944," Sally Allen McNall's "Onset," Amy Vaniotis's "Fallen Marine," and Benjamin Myers's comparison of Agincourt and Afghanistan in "Agincourt"—each takes a hard look at burning and loss, lends a perspective that is new and fresh.

In fiction as well as poetry, we also experience, within these covers, specific geographic locations from which to view the world: Catherine Browder's story "Departures" takes us from Armenia to Baku in Azerbaijan, to Moscow, to "Little Mogadishu," Missouri, where the protagonist begins to accept the kindness of her Muslim host and the Tall Grass Prairie as the sea she longs for—as home.

Slovenia, Russia, Akaroa, Provence, the frenzy of Tahrir Square in Egypt are represented with the detail and color of a painting reflecting back the impressionistic or photo-realistic view of each neighborhood, each haystack. And we are reminded through William Winfield Wright's "The View from Space," James Zimmerman's "The Dream about the Plane," and Emily Benson's vision that there is a "Problem" even with "Paradise."

Certainly, paradise is lost in the culture clash viewed by Jose Trejo-Mayo in "Chilam Balam," in Stan Zumbiel's "Eddie Autumn and His Trio," and in LaTanya McQueen's "On the Terra Roxa Earth We Saw Stars." But a trace of the lost beauty remains, with the lacemaker in Nadine Sabra Meyer's poem, who makes coarse cloth bloom.

Music, as in E. Louise Beach's "Ombra mai fù" and memory are ways of seeing, sometimes with new clarity. The humor and wisdom of Clark Smith's "The Bald Guy," Jane Vincent Taylor's "On the Train, Traveling South, Looking North" traveling backwards, and Martin Ott's "grizzled man" who wrote with his fist in steam; John Surowiecki making his sister "laugh"; and Mekeel McBride's "What If," and Dwayne Thorpe's "Noon Whistle" all encompass the sounds that are memory's vision.

And sometimes, sometimes, the view is so deeply imbedded inside, as in Kathryn Nuernberger's "*The Symbolical Head* (1883) as When Was the Last Time," so desperate in its search to "discover the soul in the body," the secret in the "pineal gland" or the "vena cava," that one fails to see the essential, the thing itself. And, as every poet worth reading reminds us, it is the something that exists outside ourselves that occasions poetry—and we are the better for it.

Nimrod International Journal
THE NIMROD LITERARY AWARDS

First Prize: $2,000
Second Prize: $1,000

POETRY: ONE LONG POEM OR SEVERAL SHORT POEMS (3-10 PAGES)
FICTION: 7,500 WORDS MAXIMUM

No previously published works or works accepted elsewhere. Omit author's name on manuscript. Include a cover sheet containing major title and subtitles of the work, author's name, address, phone, and e-mail. "Contest Entry" should be clearly marked on envelope. Manuscripts will not be returned. Include SASE for results only. *Nimrod* retains the rights to publish any contest submission. Works not accepted for publication will be released. Winners and selected finalists will be published. Works must be in English or translated by original author. Entrants must have a US address. **Entry Fee**: $20, includes one-year subscription (2 issues).

Postmark Deadline: April 30th of each year

NIMROD LITERARY CONTEST
University of Tulsa
800 S. Tucker Dr.
Tulsa, OK 74104
www.utulsa.edu/nimrod
nimrod@utulsa.edu

SUBSCRIBE TO *NIMROD* FOR JUST $18.50 (1 YEAR) OR $32.00 (2 YEARS).

Leslie Ringold, photograph

ROBIN CHAPMAN

Hubble Maps Dark Matter

Dark clumps that we can neither see nor hear,
23% of the mass of our universe,
all that we can't bring to consciousness—
that visible universe where our starry
galaxies of heat and light, our dim planets
and dust and gas shine back, build up
our world of sight from photon flight
and ricochet—has finally been found
by Hubble's eye, looking for the places
where the gravity of exploded scatter-stuff
is great enough to bend the light passing by—
and there it hides, dark matter filigreeing
space and pulling all the starry sky
along its dense scaffolding—teaching us
how to see what we cannot see
by the way it warps and bends our lives.

April 1: Madison

Dear Ones—moon past full for lamp
and I wake to one bird singing in dawn's
still dark—a cardinal, young, perhaps,
and eager as I am for the readiness
of spring, its ice-sprung lakes, its raft
of ducks—there, yesterday,
in University Bay, its water open
to scaups' white backs; and in the empty
branches of the oaks we found what could be
soft fluffs of gray pillows or grocery bags
blowing in the wind high up—except
their eyes, their telescopic vision, day-
dimmed, saw us one blur among the rest;
and their ears, asymmetric, that could hear
a mouse's heartbeat under snow,
must have heard ours thudding to see
three great-horned owls paused here
on migratory journey.

And now the daffodils that opened
only yesterday are scenting the air
and the white day-stars of bloodroot
buzz with small bees come from nowhere
and under out sticky schefflera houseplants
a steady trail of ants, come to the sugar
the aphids leave. How can we sleep
through such sweet overturnings?

Karina Borowicz

Edges

Cold and silver now
night has the thinnest
razor's edge to it
no longer the thick fragrant yellow
of wax and honey

and on the blade of morning
the bees are dying off
I see one in its dying
moving slowly as stiffening wax
clinging with its soft might
to a flower's dried center

the bee's furred body
barely distinguishable
from the zinnia's hardened fur
bristling with seed

From the collection of the Editor, photograph

Eric Pankey

Essay on Idleness

after James Turrell

Clear sky,
        but somewhere a shrug of thunder.
The book of noon opens:

Disclosure and redaction on facing pages.

Blue sky like a thrush egg,
Like the underside of a rose leaf.
                            No. The blue of beryl.
No, a drop of breast-milk on an infant's cheek,
Flax-flower blue. . . .

Clear sky. A drift of loose spider silk.

Lizard on the serpentine stonewall
Wedges into a crevice.

Somewhere a shrug of thunder.
Somewhere a crow,
                sent by the gods to fetch
The summer rain from sacred springs,

As it waits for figs to ripen.

June Depression

Once the errant cloud moves on, the sky will heal over.

Today, tomorrow: two sentences hitched by a semicolon.

Although the bees are fire amid blossoms, I carry my depression like a bag of ice in winter.

Hemmed in on both sides by ellipses, an hour lasts longer than it ought.

How rare happiness: a white fox born of a snowdrift.

The past? Back there at an impossible distance.

Mark Weiss, photograph

Dismantling the Hive

It began with one bee
unrelenting above the sink, then another
at the window. It began again
months later when he climbed the ladder, peered
through the hatch, saw only hive. All spring the bees' labor
a deniable murmur, now the attic choked by comb, its weight
bearing down on every room, the threat of hidden glistening.
Bitter his hand boring into the amber sweet that had overtaken them.
How many jars of honey could he have filled. Instead he newspapered out
brick after crystal brick, trying to return the attic to simple darkness, thinking
how he'd ignored the low drone and now had to pry
the kingdom from the house, this coffin hive a small empire
he passed down to her in viscid fistfuls, none of it spared.

Cow Tipping

What if it wasn't true? What if they tiptoed into the field
only barely, never reached the sleeping beasts? It was dark enough
to believe anything. I was scared enough, watching guard in the old Civic, to trust
they'd breached more than the "no trespassing" sign.

What was fear worth, and angst, and that feeling of abandon,
if only for a farce? If the sweat was real,
does it matter if for years I told the story as if I'd witnessed
this bold act, when not a single cow had fallen?

Mark Weiss, photograph

Into Illinois

Every July we crossed the Great River of America
into my father's childhood: porch swing, chocolate shake,
an ashtray on every table. We caught

lightning bugs in jars, took turns holding the Lab's leash
on walks to the pharmacy and back. My uncle
trimmed his rosebushes. I hid

from my grandmother's wigs, which hung,
headless, from bathroom hooks.
She had a drawer full of Kit-Kats. She played Uno.

Once, she fell asleep with a lit cigarette
and the mattress caught fire.

Back home, we didn't have a second floor or a footed tub,
no phosphorescent flies or caterpillars fuzzing the path.

In the store a block away where he sold glasses,
my uncle's goldfish grew to fit its ten-gallon tank.

A place becomes magical for the wrong reasons, or at least,
the magic complicates with time. I thought we started camping nearby
because we liked the outdoors; didn't understand

it was a choice not to stay on the couch. In that house
with its liver and mice, secrets simmered behind olive drapes—
but I built Lincoln Log mansions and chased the yard

with mason jars, oblivious to the late nights, to fights
over prescriptions and bills, to why my father didn't rebecome
the Quincy boy from photos but spent a good part of every visit

trying to fix the house he'd left. The truth thickens.
The memories are no longer as I made them.
We visited less and less. The last time, after widespread floods, we flew.

When the pilot said, *Put your hand to the window,* I did:
the river had swollen beyond my palm. My index
was the average width of the Mississippi.

Eden

I know what it's like.

One year Dad grafted branches from five
different apple varieties onto a single trunk.
The next spring he set his camera
for time-lapsed photos. Blossoms in motion.

In a succession of summers, peach seedlings
from stones Mom buried sprouted, thrived, defied
the cut of Mr. Stanisch's lawnmower and
set forth fruit we carried to all the neighbors.

I long for a garden abundant as Mom's,
perfect as Dad's. Imagine my own tiny plot
with more than perennial chives and hearty mint.

I add pepper plants, hot and sweet,
ask myself, how much room can parsley take?
What about piney rosemary?
Surely space still for a single
heirloom tomato seedling.

Among the plants I set an antiqued marker—HERBS.
For Mother's Day, my children thought I'd like two more—
    FREEDOM   JUSTICE

Before anything blossoms, before
it even blushes, before green springs
tall, plumps up, out, full beyond promise

I dream—no, I taste—perfect fruit.

Recall

the moon over Madison
almost full yet distant.

Heart-shaped balloons, each on a string,
some strings more secure than others.

One angles up, up, and away.

All my heroes, too, are gone,
dead or otherwise buried.

Others say they are with us, they are
with us. They are with, oh, no, without,

beyond us. Well-groomed,
they preen themselves

in front of cameras. They have dry hearts
or hearts filled with helium.

On the ground we find
the going tough.

Myra Shapiro

I am a Tree. Look at Me.

A tree never screams this,
which is not to say
the drama of its life,
blazing yellow from fall
to fall, shaking
openly for months
on end, perhaps wild
in massive forests,
occurs without a language.
Our minds may fail to comprehend
the vocabulary of hairy buds
bursting from having lived invisibly,
catkin blossoms giving themselves
to loll, then leaf
not singly but compounded
five or seven broad and fragrant times,
showing teeth
along green pendant edges,
laughing mockernuts,
bitternuts—those tricksters—
and glorious pecans
in thin, winged husks. Generosity
we surely see; then we cut it
down to size, hearing—*sugar me*
for your pies, my sisters' bodies
for the handles of your axes.

The Story of a Plant

I. *What Was Salvaged*

Hopeless romantics. At the nursery we paid a dollar
for the stick labeled *Blackberry Vine*, marked down
because of its near lifeless condition:

brown, docile thing, nearly over the edge of fall.
And when we asked what its chances were
the lady just shrugged, wished us luck.

So we planted it out front, said if it lived
through the winter we would keep it,
take it with us wherever we went.

II. *When We Went*

In the spring it grew, tremulous at first,
but within a month its implacable spires of green leafage
climbed waist high

as if it were acutely aware of how close it had come
to the compost heap, that great churning
it rose up from. And we made good when the time came,

dug it up again, rinsed the soil from its roots,
wrapped it in newspaper, sprayed it hourly as we crossed
the desert, kept it somehow from drying out.

III. *Bucket*

Even though it survived the journey, this is not the story
of a plant. This is the story about the survival of memory,
of carrying something that's heavier than it looks.

This is the story of a bucket filled with blackberries,
the one I brought home as a kid after picking
through thorns for hours, bloodied, in order

to fill a single ready-made pie crust, to let it cool
while we prayed over dinner,
one eye on the Lord, the other somewhere else.

Julianna McCarthy

In the Bedroom

May I wait in the tunnel of the moon's
eclipse, find in the obvious shadows
an obvious truth; small things can cast long
shadows may listen maybe are creeping here
are lost snails soft in the night blooming
jasmine, songbirds flying south in darkness,
withered words, contagion, wine smell on pond
peepers out rustled in beetle-black water
why do I want, won't you, forget, come now,
slow moon sliding free into starker shapes—
when the bed, the cat sleeping there turn
rose I'll rise, set hounds of dreams to track
and find, and lay night's small things at my feet.

Darren Dirksen, *The Rebellious Child*,
prismacolor on paper, 22" x 30"

Julianna McCarthy

There Should Have Been Flowers

Before Europe vanished in the summer of 1935,
my mother & my father, both teachers, spent all
their savings to visit first Germany, then France,
& as a consolation, England. My mother, who
taught math, converted dollars to Reichsmarks,
Francs & Pounds in the Union Bank on State Street.
It was a time when one could only hope it was safe
to do such a thing, to sail on an Italian liner
to thousands of red & black flags, & hundreds
of brown-shirted children, all of which made
my mother weep; so awkwardly young, fiercely
polite, in every way exact. She knew most of them
would die soon, she feared possibly everyone
she met in Berlin & Paris & London might die
soon. She began numbly hoarding memories —

the kidnapped Ishtar Gate at the Pergamon Museum,
the beer garden on the River Spree, the August rains,
all the flags hanging sodden & limp & running between
linden trees, their heart-shaped leaves — & telling
my father please it was time & please may we go
to Paris now.   Inside the station, more flags; red sheets
with crippled crosses. From the platform the burnt-
chocolate smell of coal-fed locomotives & a long line
at the Paris gate where police checked papers & Hitler
Jugend confiscated all German currency. Learning
she would not be able to exchange their Reichsmarks
for more Francs & Pounds, my mother looked to my father,
who nodded & crossed the tracks to the arrival gates,
where he pressed into the hands of the citizens of Berlin
the price of dinner on the Rue St. Michel, or tea at the Savoy,
or tickets to the Tate Gallery *mit den besten Wünschen*
& then turning out his pockets at the gate, walked through,
his arm around my mother
who couldn't stop laughing

DANIEL LUSK

A Room in the Woods

To sit on a stone
with my back to a tree.

I have a chair and a wall.

To look away to a hillside,
rising away from a stream below.

A floor of wild oats
and false hellebore.

This is my room—the door
and windows wherever they need to be.

The odor of solitude
like peppermint, sprung
from a cribbage of holes
a woodpecker tapped in a birch.

My young friend H recalled
waking in a thatched hut.
A man of the village stood over her,
watching her sleep.

J said on Reunion Island
homes have no doors,
and people meander like cousins
in and out of one another's houses.

Claw marks of a grizzly bear
etched the door of DB's cabin in Arlee.

"Intimacy," "privacy"—these
are meaningless without the word "door."

I draw pouch and pipe
from my pockets, a match
to spend a solemn hour.

I always imagined living alone
in the maid's room
of a brownstone on 63rd Street.

Now the cat is dead
and one less heart beating in the house.

I read somewhere
that rue was called "meadow rue"
to ease the regret.

From the collection of the Managing Editor, photograph

When Horses Love

—for my father

When horses love, it seems
an immense thing passes—obsession, war,
conversion, coming of age, revolution or
a prairie storm—

wind lashing crowns of oaks and maples,
gold and scarlet flags, virgin oats
and rye threshed green in the fields
by hail like shards of glass,
wild pounding of the haymow doors.

And watching them stamp and whistle
we might be afraid
but there is too much of wonder.

It is the same in heart-racing weather,
roof beat and mutter of falling water,
runoff in the gutters,
rain larruping the flailing branches.

Blowing in the open window,
lifting the curtains,
sweat-wet on the page where I write.

Thunderstorms were metaphors
for wildness I knew our father felt,
heartache and regret and turmoil inside.

He watched them come, great
towering spinnakers of rampant thunderclouds,
roil, and churn, and billow, a gathering
madness above us over the westward pasture.

The two of us stood, larger
and small,
awestruck, apart,
faces canted to the expanding skies.

Mare and stallion at a reckless gallop,
wheeling at the fences,
manes and tails flying, teeth bared
to neck and haunch and withers,
rearing to paw the wind.

Screaming.

Sometimes at night,
he stood on the wide porch
or at the open windows, unmoving.
Lightning cleaved the dark.
Thunder rocked the house.

While our mother roused us
from our beds upstairs, hearts hammering,
scrawny-legged in our underwear,
shepherded into dank safety of the coal bin
in the washing cellar,

he stared, transfixed,
and smoke curled outward
from his cigarette as from a lighted fuse.

Sometimes a sound surrounded us,
crowding our chests to hurt,
shutting our throats

as if thunder spoke,
as if some voice within,
as if some resonance returned the rumbling
as human song.

I never asked
what made him weep and sing.
Or why life seemed so ordinary otherwise.

How the Story Begins: Prelude to a Ballet

A girl steps out of the trees.

What she is wearing,
her first gesture upon emerging
from these woods—these will matter
little to the story.

If she takes off her shoe,
or bends from the waist to tighten the laces.
If she adjusts her clothes—the loose
chambray shirt, or the snug cardigan.
Maybe she smoothes the seat of her trousers.

If she looks up at the sun
or at the faint disc of the moon.
Maybe shields her eyes with a hand.

Whether she glances furtively
over her shoulder
toward the woods behind her
as if she heard something—a twig snap,
or a strange, almost human bird call.

If she appears to notice
that her shirt is buttoned unevenly,
and begins to redo it,
first one button, then the next.

Suppose she begins at the bottom
to correct the mistake, each step
requiring she first unbutton
the previous, errant fastening, and so on.
As if learning the clarinet.

What if she finds at the last step, her garment
is even more askew,
and begins again, this time with the button
between her breasts, where
she was bitten by a mosquito.

It would be simpler, better
(we imagine from our seat
high on the veranda) if she simply
undid the garment altogether
to begin again.

Perhaps she removes a bottle
from her backpack and drinks long.
Wipes her hands absently
on her thighs.

If she twirls a leaf between her fingers,
or places it between her thumbs
and puts it to her lips.
Or lifts the wild blossom
she carries to her cheek.

If she begins to run begins
to walk quickly aimlessly
looks side to side, or far ahead,
looks at the ground.

Maybe a bird flies past overhead,
a gold thread in its beak. Or
the shadow of a bird with a strand
of hair. Or no bird but the shadow
of a cloud, scudding across the grass,
across her face.

If she stands still and stretches
her slender arms high over her head.
If she bends deeply from the waist,
her shirt riding open to reveal a tattoo,
her long legs partly obscured.
Fingers appearing to touch the earth.

Watching her, I believe
a hair from the head
of a comely stranger, or a pale stain
from a cheap ankle bracelet,
can change the rules of nature.

She may forget what she saw earlier
from hiding, through the limbs
of witch hazel, there among ferns,
on the bright green moss
beside the rotting tree.

Or she may remember forever
the two of them locked together,
her surprise, their fur,
their wild bird flutter,
her heart's clamor, their animal voices.

She may want to know
if it hurts, if it pleases, if it heals after.
She will smile to herself
as she is doing now.
She will deny everything.

She may take off her other shoe
and continue, barefooted,
across the broad and undulating field.

May sense me watching from above
as she advances, dancing inside
to some private music,
a little spring at the knees.

Perhaps her arms are extended
generously, palms up, to show
how she herself might surrender.
How she might carry a newborn.
Might carry the dead.

Vanished Reflections

Memory is one way the world rids itself of us.
    How she was in the beginning . . .
When we move forward, I tell her, something will always be left back.
That's the way it is with the girl.
    The girl: What is it she wants to tell me?
Beneath the pier, its planks washed by salt air, she sits.
waiting for her salvation, waiting for my writing.

    If I can find the problem to solve,
the puzzle, the argument, I can replace her sorrow
with a brilliant diffusion/illusion of who she is.

    Look at her wanting me to write
about an apple. And then eating it instead. What can
possibly happen, with such behavior?

    Writing is about consequence, I tell her,
and she is like the wind
    pitching in all directions. Now there she goes
walking through dead grasses, high at her waist.
    Now she dissolves into her own reflection.

    Persistence with the past negotiates her life.
Sometimes she wants me to write
    a single word for *dream* again and again
papered over with her emotions.
    I am not sentimental
but she stains everything she touches with tears.

    She says she will haunt me until I feel something.
I say I will not be stalked by a dream guided by her imaginings.

Her allure is something that cannot be caught,
things invisible only the seer can see.
    Now she is under the apple tree.
Now she's the bird in the tree,
    Now the feathers.
If you believe in someone enough,
Time's sweet crawl will bring her back.
    She comes only so she can leave.
    She comes for that.

The Nature of the Correspondence and the Required Heroics

The nature of a poem
requires an attempt at heroics.
A storm steps to the horizon and rattles
the sky each time you wake
from a nightmare alone in bed.

And the nature of a call to the heart?
The circus clown sits in the middle of a tent.
The bright red of the lips has worn off.
The big, round nose is missing.
He's playing spoons on his knees.
Civilization is a dance step
always in need of new music.

The nature of a pause, again,
this is about you.
You fall back to sleep
humming a song.
It's a false sort of courage
but right now any courage will do.

Every letter of the alphabet
was once a soldier armed with a pike
marching through a muddy field.
Read any story close enough,
you can track the letters back to the field.

Ex Cathedra

What no one knows about me
is that my left ear is made of rubber.
The original was lost in an accident
when I was nineteen. As Dr. Gorlick
sewed the new one to the side of my head
he said it needed to be replaced
every eleven years to appear to age
along with my face. Vanity compels me
to replace it every thirteen.
A rubber ear isn't as uncommon as you think.
One president and two movie stars each had a rubber ear.
The actors appeared together in a movie
without knowing about the other's prosthesis.
Each morning I apply a lotion to the ear
so the rubber doesn't discolor. Cell by cell,
the body replaces itself every seven years.
It's simple science. I lay on my side
as Dr. Gorlick sewed. A nurse held the ear in position.
Lidocaine and something I don't remember
prevented me from feeling the blood
run down my neck and cheek.
But I could taste it and began to spit.
The nurse put gauze pads
between my lips and apologized.
Things like this happen all the time.
Someone bleeds, someone apologizes.

CATHERINE BROWDER

Departures

The exodus took place during Alina Naroyan's first decade as an American. One by one her friends and countrymen left the apartments in Kansas City, some joining children in far-flung suburbs, while Alina stayed put. She had no children, and her closest émigré relative lived in Texas. When he invited her to join his family, she considered it briefly and then refused. She'd never been dependent on anyone and couldn't imagine starting now. Besides, friends had warned her about Texas: *Don't go, Lina. It's too hot!* (As if it weren't miserable enough in Missouri!) Then a wave of new refugees swept into the apartment complex, and Alina thought she might drown.

First to go was a neighbor who'd attended Alina's citizenship party, a quiet woman with a sick husband. Alina had come down to the entry to collect her mail and found Linda collecting hers. "We're moving," she whispered. "The end of the month."

"Where?" Alina asked. She had no sense of her adopted city and had never driven a car.

"Assisted living," said Linda soberly with a nod of the head. "A place in Independence. I need help with Frank."

Alina sorted through the pieces of this news bulletin. *Assisted living?* Linda explained. *Independence?* She thought it might have something to do with freedom, but from what? Again Linda explained. *Ah, that Independence!* Alina knew this to be the next town over, only a few miles east of where they stood, in the foyer of a declining brick building now infused with the spices of Africa.

Six months later Luba, who once lived upstairs, relocated downtown to a tall apartment building favored by retired Americans where, Luba pridefully pointed out, the language of choice was English. Alina was not saddened to see Luba go since Luba confronted her new life (her previous one, too, Alina guessed) with monumental scorn. Never a kind word from Luba, or a flicker of curiosity. Next, darling Nina, who'd become like a daughter, took her own little girl and went to live with a brother in Raytown.

But on the day Stella stopped by, bringing a container of *borscht,* Alina's heart sank.

"We've found a place," Stella said. "In Overland Park."

Kansas again. It was Stella who drove her to the Russian store or to the Price Chopper when it rained, also to the doctor's, even once to see the ballet perform the Nutcracker. Stella was now a nurse—in Kansas—and when she moved she would take an entire household with her. When that day arrived, Alina realized, she would be the only European left in the building.

After Stella's visit, Alina went to her bedroom and lay down. Her journey had taken her farther than she would ever have imagined. Too far, perhaps—from Baku by the sea to Moscow to the exact center of the United States, to a city she had scarcely known existed. Nowadays, when she opened the sliding door to her balcony, she could not hear a single word of English or Russian, Armenian or Azerbaijani, for that matter. The area was no longer the comfortable hodgepodge it had once been. By 2007 and in her 77th year, she was the only one of her countrymen who remained in what she now thought of as Little Somalia. An Armenian forced to flee Azerbaijan for her life, Alina was again surrounded by Muslims, and she pondered whether her journey ought to continue.

※ ※ ※

In her former life she'd been a musician, the arc of her career utterly predictable. Her mother had been Alina's first piano teacher. Early on the young family had moved from Yerevan, Armenia, to the neighboring Republic of Azerbaijan, so her father might teach at a better school. But that was in the old Soviet days when everything worked and anyone could safely live anywhere—before Gorbachev got it into his head to split the Union apart and The Trouble began.

After training in Moscow, she returned to the Music Institute in Baku as a piano instructor. Even then, Baku was one of the most secular and open Islamic societies, where music and opera and fine arts flourished, where visitors could find Persian carpets, caviar. and Western theatre. She had accompanied several of the most prominent singers in the region, including mezzo-soprano Vera Ivanova. Then the great Portuguese soprano Pilar da Silva arrived as a visitor to the Music Institute, having left her own country during a time of distress, staying on to teach and perform and become one of Alina's closest friends. Alina was 40 and still single when Vera introduced her to the tenor Bruno Dorn, son of a Russian father and an Azeri mother, ten years Alina's senior, and divorced. Her brief marriage to Bruno stood out as the best decade of her life, until he'd died of an aneurysm—like Caruso—long before The Trouble forced her to flee. Even her good friends from student days had scattered: Natalia to Israel, and Sonya off to Germany.

The knowledge that Azerbaijanis and Armenians had always fought lived on in one small ancestral pocket of her mind, even though she'd never been affected. She preferred to remember the good years of the Soviet Union when the government maintained order, ethnicity took a backseat, and people got on with their lives. Then came *perestroika* . . . . Why was it that after 60 years of civility the world went crazy?

When The Trouble first began, a sympathetic neighbor had told her, "They probably could not care less about you. It's your apartment they're after." The same large apartment the government had granted her teacher father and she'd continued to live in after her parents' deaths. In those Soviet days, an apartment could remain in the family in perpetuity. The rent was not only low, but also controlled. One evening she heard voices in the hallway and later she began seeing the angry faces during the day. She'd spent most of her life in that temperate city on the Caspian but would never be considered a native. When ugly threats were slipped under her door, she packed two suitcases, all the goods she could carry, and all the mementos worth saving. She carried her bags to her neighbor Nikolai's apartment, and he and his Russian wife took her in. A Tatar from Tajikistan, Nikolai was so fierce-looking no Azeri would bother him. Their blood lust was reserved for Armenians, not for Tatars or ethnic Russians. Alina had heard the screams in the night even before she fled.

"They" pounded on Nikolai's door while Alina hid in the closet. Someone must have seen her flee. The Tatar finally opened up, the chain still attached, while his wife cowered in the kitchen. *Are you crazy?* Alina heard his voice from the depths of the closet, behind the winter coats. *Are you nuts? I am here with my wife and you are upsetting her. I don't like that. So go away. And if you come back, you'll get this.* He shook a length of steel pipe. She knew this because he showed it to her later. She spent the daylight hours in the closet since "their" eyes and ears were everywhere, even in the apartment below.

Three days in the closet.

Alina slept on a bed of coats, a boot for a pillow. She did not move until the dead of night when she crept through the dark to the toilet and bathed her body with a cloth, for "they" were listening. After three days, an official arrived—sent by an influential cousin in Moscow. At dusk this official escorted her from Nikolai's apartment and drove her to the pier. He came with an official car and an official bodyguard and because he was an Azeri, no one dared to accost them. Her cousin had arranged passage on the night ship across the Caspian, and from there she traveled by train to Moscow.

Alina never saw Nikolai or his wife again, nor the Azeri official, and she owed them her life. Only later did she hear about the "massacres," passed on by word of mouth from one horrified Armenian to the next: Someone had heard the BBC broadcast over a wireless, the mob that stormed a hospital in a northern city, tossing patients and babies out of windows. She'd always hoped it was only a rumor, but when she reached Kansas City and met other Armenian-Azerbaijanis, she learned it was true. It seemed so odd, shocking really, that her English teachers hadn't heard about the massacres. She asked her friend Jeanne-Marie about this omission. A Frenchwoman married to an American, Jeanne-Marie rolled her eyes and threw up her hands. "What do you expect, Lina? The Americans want that Caspian oil." Then the Bosnian horrors eclipsed anything that had occurred in distant Baku.

What made people so wicked? She'd lived peaceably among Azerbaijanis most of her life. If the Soviet Union were still intact, she would still be in the same apartment she'd lived in all her life, a woman with a good life and good work, with friends and pets. Instead she took her considerable savings and the support offered by the U.S. government, and left. Now all that remained of that life were a few photos hanging on her new walls and one album, her life condensed to what she could carry. As for the cats and piano... well, she'd had to leave them, and run.

❊ ❊ ❊

She found the tired old upright at the City Union Thrift for $100, an inferior piano in need of new felts. When one runs for her life, she joked with Jeanne-Marie, one cannot bring along her baby grand. She located a tuner and put the instrument into passable shape so she could practice without cringing.

She'd even called the Conservatory of Music. They were polite, marginally interested, but alas, she knew, her English was not good enough, nor her credentials up to scratch. Besides, they'd just hired a flashy young pianist, a Van Cliburn finalist from the former Soviet Union. There would be room for only one "Russian" in this conservatory, even though neither of them was Russian—the young prizewinner was an Uzbek.

❊ ❊ ❊

The Garcias phoned to say they could not attend English School that night, or the night after. "So sorry, Alina. We'll pick you up next week." She accepted this as the price of being a passenger, of having no car in car-hungry America. A bus passed conveniently near the apartment, but after class she didn't want to wait on the Avenue in the dark. She did not like the look of the people loitering near the bus stop, so reluctantly she would forego English class for the week. Until she saw the taxi in the parking lot behind the building. For two days she went periodically to the landing to see if she could discover who in the building drove the cab.

On the third day of her vigil she saw below her a tall, lean Somali leaving the apartment where Stella's family once lived. He walked down the three concrete steps to the lot, and into the taxi. She followed quickly, tightening her brown wool cardigan around her. He'd just started the car when she waved at him. He flashed a friendly smile and rolled down the window.

"Yes, Madame." He turned off the engine and to her amazement climbed out of his cab.

"I live in your building. Let me introduce myself." She held out her hand, and then quickly withdrew it. Was he one of those Muslims who still followed the old ways and did not shake hands? Probably. He had not stopped smiling, and she gazed at his perfect teeth.

"Miss Alina," he said and nodded his head in a little bow. "So happy to meet you. I am Abdi, and I have seen you before." He nodded his head again and placed his right hand over his heart.

"I had a question," she said and explained her transportation problem.

Yes, he knew where the school was. His wife Khalida attended the school some mornings, and Alina widened her eyes.

"Really?" she exclaimed, relieved to discover a wife. "I will stop by."

How serviceable and clear his English sounded. She had little trouble understanding him. It was her English that was fading from lack of use.

"This is business," she added, pointing to the taxi. "I will pay you."

He closed his eyes and waved his hand in front of his face as if swatting flies, his lips pursing. "I shall take you to school Monday, and I shall pick you up after." He bowed slightly. "We are neighbors...."

On Saturday she prepared the walnut rolls, so popular with her American friends, carefully rolling the flour, adding the butter and sugar and chopped nuts. After baking, she wrapped them in foil and placed them in the fridge. On Sunday, she dressed carefully in a dark printed long-sleeved dress, a scarf at her throat, and went down to the landing to verify that Abdi's taxi was not in service but parked in the lot. There were, in fact, two taxis parked on the far side, and for a moment she felt perplexed. She had no idea which taxi was his, but taxis had become a cottage industry among the Somalis. She would have to risk it. She returned to her apartment and took the walnut rolls from the fridge, tightening the foil around the plate and took the stairs down to the apartment that had once been Stella's. She knocked and waited. She heard movement within and the piping voice of a child, but no one came to the door. Alina knocked louder. She heard a woman's voice trilling inside, two female voices in fact, and wondered which one was Abdi's wife. Perhaps there was also a mother. She knocked a third time but the voices carried on and then someone inside called out something but not in English and she called back, "It's Alina." All voices stopped.

The door flung open and there stood Abdi, smiling with his perfect teeth. He clasped his hands together and exclaimed, "Miss Alina! Welcome to my family." He stepped aside and ushered her in. She marveled at how tall he was, everything about him elongated and cylindrical, even his high forehead, and glossy black. A pleasant-looking man, perhaps in his thirties.

He said something speedily to the two women who appeared to be moving between kitchen and living room. "Our neighbor Bibi, and this is Khalida." He gestured toward an extremely young woman with enormous eyes, who stepped forward. "My wife," he added. She was dressed like all the women in her building—*hidden*, Alina thought—pulling a headscarf hastily around her face, more yards of colorful cloth draped over her body. When she stepped forward, Alina saw that she was hugely pregnant. Alina offered her the plate: "Russian pastries." Did this young woman speak English? Alina went on anyway. When she paused, Abdi interpreted, and the girl nodded, stepped forward and received the plate, then handed the plate to her friend, took both Alina's hands in hers and said, "Thank you." At least Alina thought these were the words that came out. With Khalida speaking in Somali and Abdi in English, they asked her to sit. As she turned she saw for the first time the little girl hanging on to her father's pant leg.

"And this is little Fatima," Abdi said.

Alina bent down to greet her, and the child frowned and darted behind him, hiding her face in his leg.

Alina turned back to the lovely young woman. "And when is the baby due?"

* * *

She was prompt that first Monday—Jeanne-Marie was forever scolding her for being late—dressed and seated in her living room and fretful he might have forgotten. At 5:45, Abdi knocked on her door. "Miss Alina," he called. "Time for English."

The trip took less than five minutes, down Garfield to the Avenue, west past the Paseo and the entrance to the highway, beside a clutch of grim public housing she never liked to pass on foot, over the bridge and another highway entrance—so many highways—and right again. The English School was housed in an old recreation and community center, built, she was told, by other immigrants, Italian stonemasons who'd once lived in the nearby buildings and attended the Catholic church.

Abdi hopped out and opened the door. "I will be back at 9 p.m."

Throughout the evening she couldn't focus on the lesson, her thoughts drifting, worried that she might have to wait alone and forgotten in the dark. Yet when she left the building that evening, the taxi was parked at the curb. Her heart lifted in relief. She walked to the passenger side and tapped at the window. He was listening to the radio and waved, switching the radio off. He popped out, moved quickly around the front, and opened the front passenger door.

"Please," Alina implored. "No need to get out."

"But you are my guest."

She climbed in back, wondering if she should have gotten in front. That would alter the relationship, she thought, make it too personal. When they returned to the parking lot of their apartment building, she reached over the back seat. "I would like to pay you."

"No, no, no," he protested, his head wagging vehemently. "It is my pleasure to take you to school. Khalida used to go, you know, but now she is in her ninth month—not so good."

"But you are a businessman," she insisted. "And this is your business."

His head continued to shake, his hand flying up into that universal gesture of refusal. From her handbag Alina removed an envelope with a five-dollar bill inside and implored him to take it. The twin gestures of insistence and refusal threatened to lengthen out, and Alina placed the envelope on the front seat. Abdi grabbed the envelope and swiftly tucked it inside her still open purse.

"Thank you," she said in surrender.

Abdi bowed his head. "You are always my guest."

The Garcias phoned Wednesday evening to tell her they would not be returning to school after all. They had good news: they were moving. *Carlos has found a good job!* How excited they were but sad to say good-bye. Cradling the phone after their call, Alina wondered if returning to the English School was something she needed to do. But where else could she shore up her disintegrating English? Where else would she see her friends? Now everyone in the apartment building was Somali, and a great sense of loneliness swept over her. Not that they weren't pleasant, as it turned out, but their children were so loud and numerous, playing ball outside her windows, calling and laughing and disturbing her peace. She would now have to approach Abdi and talk business this time. For a day she planned her English words carefully, picking and throwing out and choosing again the words that might appeal to a young father. She prepared a plateful of Russian *pierogis*, filled with potato and cabbage and butter, surrounded by a ring of Russian chocolates, wrapped in colorful foil. As she descended the stairs to the ground floor, she coached herself: *This is business. Business!*

※ ※ ※

Every Monday and Thursday for a month Abdi took her

to the English School until Khalida had her baby. On that day a strange woman knocked on her door, wreathed in scarves and a long draping garment in a colorful print. If you could not discern a human shape, Alina thought, a face shone like a beacon.

"The baby has come," the woman said in a clear, scarcely accented English.

"Khalida and Abdi's baby?" Alina forced herself to look carefully at the woman's face. She appeared to be in her thirties. Her features were well proportioned, her eyes large and intelligent, her mouth trim, eyebrows plucked. She thought perhaps she'd seen this woman at the English School. She felt certain this woman had been educated before she arrived in this country, unlike sweet Khalida.

"Yes. Abdi asked that I tell you he could not take you to class this evening."

Alina nodded. *Of course*. "What happy news! Is everyone well? The mother? The child?"

"I do not know," the woman said. "But we are hopeful. Allah be praised."

The woman said her impeccable goodbyes and left. *Allah be praised?* A shiver ran along the skin of Alina's neck and scalp, and she felt besieged by the dismaying sense of isolation that now defined her days. Who was left but herself? What had once been laughingly referred to as Little Baku had changed so drastically it now replicated, in speech and look, the Horn of Africa.

※ ※ ※

"We've named him Hassan," Abdi said, as he drove Alina to English class the following week.

"And he is healthy?" Alina asked.

"Very. Strong lungs. Good stomach."

"And Khalida? She's well?"

"Hassan's mother is doing well."

What a curious way to refer to one's wife. She wondered if Khalida had been elevated in some manner, or simply redefined: the mother of a boy. A universal event, it seemed, since boys were assumed to be better. She'd never embraced the notion that the birth of a son should be more cause for celebration than a daughter. It didn't seem to matter in her expatriate community. Among her countrymen, daughters were equally plentiful and attentive (or inattentive) to their mothers, although this was not something she could speak to with any authority. She'd never dwelt on it, until recently, as the months and then years flew off the calendar and she found herself celebrating yet another birthday. A relic, that's what she was. She still dyed her hair, the preferred henna staining her hands. She still polished her nails and rouged her cheeks and surrounded herself with her younger Russian, Ukrainian, and Kazakh friends from the English School. The young people had replaced the aging ones who'd moved to the suburbs and allowed themselves to grow old. Oh, so many she'd lost touch with!

But what should she give the baby? She asked Jeanne-Marie, who was never at a loss for an opinion. When she inquired, Jeanne-Marie shrugged in that peculiarly annoying Gallic manner with her face puckered, eyes fluttering shut, shoulders hunching. It wasn't like Jeanne-Marie to hold back. "Well, you can't very well give a doll."

Alina importuned the young Kazakhs to drive her to the Russian store. Here she bought the little Russian bear of carved wood, plus the metal top that spun when you pushed the plunger in the middle. There had been so few children in her life. Bruno had a daughter from his previous marriage, but the girl was grown by the time Bruno married Alina. She did not remember any Azeri customs for children, and the Armenian ones most certainly would not apply. So the wooden bear that "played" the wooden bells when you pulled the little string, plus the top—these would have to do. Alina wrapped the toys carefully in bright blue tissue paper and placed then in a gift bag that looked suspiciously like Christmas wrapping.

She waited another week before considering a visit to the young family, as much out of confusion as consideration. When, exactly, did Somali people call? Should she come into the busy apartment or deliver her gift from the threshold? The young family would likely have little rest with a crying infant in the house. Suddenly she remembered the little girl. Two toys for the baby boy and nothing for little Fatima? How unfair! She went to the dresser in her bedroom and pulled out the bottom drawer where she kept assorted trinkets and toys she'd picked up at the Russian store— hostess gifts, holiday gifts. She searched among the scarves and small decorative spoons until she found the little nested *matryoshka* doll: five dolls altogether, one inside the other. The main doll was too blond and Slavic for Alina's taste, but she was beautifully decorated with a lovely red scarf and elaborate dress and apron painted over her round doll's body; and Alina wrapped it in a shard of yellow tissue. Then with wavering conviction, she went downstairs to Abdi's apartment and knocked on the door.

She was reminded of her first visit: she heard activity within but no one seemed to acknowledge the door. She knocked louder, fearful she might waken the babe. There was still no answer. She would try once again and then leave, giving her gift to Abdi when she saw him next. The door suddenly flung open, startling her, and the woman who had come to announce the baby's birth stood there like a solemn and burnished gatekeeper. Then the stern expression vanished, and the woman smiled. "Ah, it's you! Please come in."

She took Alina by the arm, raising her voice to speak to someone in another room, and then insisted that Alina take a seat. It hadn't occurred to her that Abdi would probably be working. She heard voices in the bedroom, and then Khalida and the baby emerged. Alina rose to greet them, the other woman translating for the new mother. How beautiful the little boy was, so small and perfect, his eyes sleepy.

"He has just finished his dinner," the tall woman said. "But Khalida wanted you to meet him."

Alina glanced around the living room: only two chairs and a misshapen coffee table, with numerous large cushions on the carpeted floor. The two women insisted that she sit down again, in the plumper of the two chairs. She recognized the imperatives of their hospitality because they so much resembled her own. Before she sat she held up the holiday bag. "There are two gifts for Hassan… and one for your daughter."

The neighbor translated for Khalida and took the handle of the bag out of Alina's outstretched hand. Khalida thanked her and bowed her head. The reception of the gifts struck Alina as strangely solemn, as if to trill or titter over the gift might demean it, and their appreciation, and she felt moved by their gravitas. The tall woman disappeared into the galley kitchen with the gift bag, leaving Alina alone with mother and babies. Alina admired the baby again and spoke to the little girl, knowing whatever she said would be lost on Khalida. When the older woman returned, she was carrying a tray of tea.

❖ ❖ ❖

Several weeks after little Hassan's birth, Luba called to inform Alina that space was opening up in her building downtown. Luba arranged to pick her up for a visit and sat beside Alina as she filled in the forms. There was a waiting list, the manager regretted to inform her. The Tower Apartments were very popular with retirees, but she was certainly qualified and would be considered. Alina returned home feeling neither encouraged nor rejected. Whatever would happen would happen. What else could one do? In the meantime, she lived as she had always lived: reading, playing her thrift store piano, attending the English School, watching Russian-language videos, and spending an inordinate amount of time on the phone. Yet whenever she paused to rest, the young Somali family crept into her mind.

For eight months her days stretched out into a predictability that had begun to make her feel stale, even elderly. In one bleak and heavy moment she contemplated a return to Moscow, then chided herself. *Lina, you are an American now. Your life is here.* Abdi continued to drive her to English class Monday and Thursday evenings (her favorite hours of the week); on Fridays she walked to the neighborhood grocery, unless her Kazakh friends drove her to the Price Chopper; once a month she had lunch with Jeanne-Marie (but Jeanne-Marie was as prickly these days as Luba); and every Saturday she gave Nina's daughter a piano lesson. She had placed a notice by the mailboxes that she was available to teach piano, but no one called or came to her door. It wasn't that she needed the money. She'd clung to her savings, and there was the reliable monthly SSI check, reserved for elderly refugees. Still she would have liked to teach someone in this new country the music she loved.

In March the Tower Apartments phoned: a one-bedroom had opened up on the third floor. Small but nice, if she was still interested. It would be available in a matter of weeks. Luba came to fetch her, and Alina viewed the rooms, the clean and carpeted corridors, the light and well-appointed ground floor lounge where one could sit and read the newspapers and watch television and visit with neighbors. It reminded her of a hotel lobby, which gave her a vacant feeling, but it was safe, if one wanted to leave one's apartment but not the building. Nonresidents had to pass through a security door that was carefully monitored. Luba took her arm and escorted her to the end of the third floor hallway. Arranged here was a sitting area with a small white wrought iron table and two matching chairs, wall-to-ceiling windows and large potted plants, overlooking a tree-lined street.

"Every floor has one," Luba said, indicating the small café table and chairs. "Nice and bright, you can have a picnic."

Alina glanced at her old friend. It wasn't like Luba to promote and applaud. Alina would have expected her to fault the sitting area for being too small or the potted palm for being too large. "And you like it here?" Alina asked.

"I do. Not perfect, but better than where you are. Everyone speaks English, you know." Luba gave her a superior look, and Alina knew what she was implying. The reminder strengthened her resolve, which had continued to waver. Unfortunately, the Tower apartment was in all ways smaller than her current place, and a quarter of the size of her Baku home, but who could have everything?

"Lina, you can walk to the opera," Luba declared. "Even the ballet!"

She signed the agreement under Luba's approving eyes but when she returned to the old place, her heart rose up in rebellion. How could she leave? The last twenty years of her life had been one departure after another. How could one live in this way? Her eyes traveled the walls hung with the paintings she'd found at the City Union thrift, the rugs she'd purchased from the Russian store, the framed photos from Baku—Bruno, Vera, Pilar. She had acquired chairs, tables, even a daybed. Second-hand, to be sure, but they were hers. She would never be able to squeeze it all in. Then the old apartment seemed to swell with seventeen years of memories. How could she bundle her American life up once more and squeeze it into an even smaller space? She walked to the upright piano and touched it. It would come with her, of course, since she had gone to the trouble of restoring it and couldn't live without it. She sat down at the instrument, stretched her fingers and began a Chopin nocturne.

She would manage, she counseled herself as she leaned into the keyboard. She had always managed. She would pare down. She had survived once before, twice if she included the decision to leave Moscow after her escape from Baku. Friends here had asked why she'd left Russia. Why indeed? Because she was an impatient and independent woman and could not bear to rely on her cousin's family. Because she had her own career and way of living, and it was not theirs. Because she was only 60 at the time and everything still seemed possible, and what was possible in America, with proffered American support, seemed far better and less cramped than anything in Moscow in its newly diminished condition, its post-Soviet confusion. Sonya had moved to Germany, after all. And Natalia had immigrated to Israel, so why not Alina Naroyan? Yes, in 1991 everything still seemed possible and interesting and adventuresome!

Alina finished the nocturne and rested her fingers over the keys. She walked into the small dining room adjacent to the kitchen and then into the spare bedroom, cataloguing what would come with her and what she must give away. She thought suddenly of Abdi and Khalida's sparsely furnished place, and began to make a mental list. They must be the first to choose.

❊ ❊ ❊

She couldn't bear to watch as Abdi and his two friends maneuvered the piano across the living room. A headache set in. She'd just had the piano tuned, and after the move she would have to tune it again. Abdi arranged for the truck, but the men were taxi drivers, not movers, and their struggle was too painful to bear. When the instrument passed through the door, lumbering slowly on its misshapen wheels, she fled into the back room and stared out the window.

Her friends had rallied: the young Kazakhs with a different truck, Nina and her brother in a large SUV, even Jeanne-Marie's husband with his minivan. Not much remained now except some clothing in a suitcase, a few toiletries, a teakettle and cup, and the bed she intended to leave behind. The piano had been the last significant piece of furniture. Abdi and Khalida had taken a small side table, a dresser, two rugs and a chair—thrillingly received them, she had to admit, and this had given her unexpected pleasure. The Kazakhs had taken another chair and rug, a few paintings. Abdi would drive her to the Tower apartment to supervise the placement of the piano, but for the moment, she could not watch. The instrument rumbled toward the stairs, and she felt the accumulated years move with it.

❊ ❊ ❊

Exhausted, Alina stood among the boxes filling the new apartment, pointing nervously here and there, her temper short. At least the piano was in its appointed space. Before he left, Abdi turned to her and flashed his astonishing smile.

"Miss Alina, would you like a beautiful ride in the country? Khalida and I would like to thank you for the furnishings. And Khalida wants to have a picnic."

"Now?" she asked in amazement. It was April and cold.

He ignored her astonishment and went on. They would drive out to a special place friends had told him about. Had she been to Kansas?

Well, of course! One could not live on the Missouri side and not at some point visit the Kansas suburbs, with the Russian store and half her friends. She wouldn't have minded living there herself, except she did not drive. And since there were few buses and no streetcars or trains, what was the point? She'd never even seen a taxi there.

"But this is farther," he told her. "Far out in the countryside. We will wait until the weather warms."

At last, on a morning in late May with wavering sunshine and a brisk breeze, Abdi and his family, packed into the taxi, arrived at the Tower Apartments at ten. Alina had dressed warmly just in case: a sweater and a light coat and scarf.

"You will sit in front, please, Miss Alina," Abdi announced. Khalida was sitting in the backseat with the babies.

Once Alina was settled, her container of walnut rolls and *pierogis* and chocolate at her feet, Abdi turned to her and announced with a grin, "Now you are riding shotgun."

She wasn't sure she'd heard him correctly. "What is this? 'Riding shotgun'?"

"It means to sit in the seat where you are now. Beside the driver."

"But what does it mean?"

He shrugged. "Who knows? An American told me. In a taxi almost nobody rides shotgun." He laughed at some joke unavailable to her.

He drove them through the city and onto the highway, traveling the edge of the metropolitan area, then onto the Interstate and at last beyond the suburbs. She had never been this far west before. They traveled for over an hour, nearly two, and then at an exchange with scarcely anything to see but farmland and one vast gas station on a corner, he drove away from the busy road and along a smaller one. She felt as if the car was plunging between rows of sprouting grain, with no idea what was growing there. She had spent her life in cities and now scarcely noticed the road signs, observing only an amazing number of unknown birds flying over the fields or perched on the wires. One large bird circled in the distance.

"Look, Miss Alina," Abdi pointed. "An eagle!"

He declared this with such authority that Alina let her gaze linger. But the bird was black against the sun. She couldn't discern any features familiar to her from paintings and posters—the talons, the beak, the stern eyes and white head. Alina shrugged.

"So, Miss Alina. How is your new apartment?"

"So-so," she said, not wishing to sound too pleased. "Smaller, you know. But my countrywomen live there. Two of them."

Abdi nodded approvingly. "That's good. Like family. Now you can speak your language."

Not exactly like family, she thought. She would never wish to consider Luba *family*.

"It's for older people. Retired people."

"Ah, and no kids. No noise." He threw back his head and chuckled.

She glanced at him as he shared her news with Khalida. She did not tell him she felt safer there, with the elaborate security system. Nor did she wish to say there were white people like herself. It would not do to explain that the gulf between them was too vast—a woman with an austere European education, who loved Dumas and Tolstoy, played Mozart and Beethoven, and watched the Bolshoi on faded videos. She did not wish to say she was not interested in these fluid, undisciplined people who cooked at 10 at night and let their many children stay up until all hours or play on the grass in front of her apartment. When the first wave of Somalis arrived, a noisy family had moved in above her, waking her at all hours. She did not wish to reveal that once, in frustration and fury, she had banged a broom handle against her ceiling and screamed in Russian, *What's the matter with you people? Are you animals?*

She'd grown fond of Abdi and his family. He had helped

her—a single woman frequently in need of help. Nor could she bring herself to say the word—*old*—or any of its English variations. She had held *old* at bay for so long until this last move, which was at last an acknowledgment: The Tower Apartments were only for retirees. For *old* people—and now in her 80th year she ought to be allowed to enjoy safety and quiet, oughtn't she?

"How did you come here?" he asked, the question popping up unexpectedly.

"How? By airplane of course."

He burst out laughing, as if she'd made a joke. "No. I meant the reason."

"Ah, well, that is a long story… I couldn't stay any more in Baku. Everything changed. A new government, you see. It wasn't safe for me."

He nodded and said something to Khalida, who looked at Alina with her deep and sympathetic eyes. He didn't ask why and she was glad. She wasn't sure her English was up to it.

"And you?" she asked. She did not usually ask questions, fearful she wouldn't understand the answers. It was so much better to talk. That way she could practice her English. But nowadays Jeanne-Marie told her she was always interrupting, never letting anyone speak. *Why are you so chatty, Lina? It's like you never want to hear an answer. And whenever anyone tries to speak, you walk right over them with your busy tongue!* But Jeanne-Marie was a talker herself. How many times had they found themselves in dueling conversations?

"You, too?" she asked him.

"Yes, we too. No government. Nothing. Like you, not safe."

She wanted to hear the rest and waited, but Abdi turned and spoke to his wife, then announced, "We are almost there."

Abdi lowered his window. The draft made Alina shudder and she asked him to raise it up, please. "Yes, in a moment. But smell the air, Miss Alina. First smell."

"Drafts are not healthy," she said, instantly regretting the overbearing tone. At one time or another non-Russian friends had registered a complaint against this imperious tone, as if it were a national flaw. Even Jeanne-Marie. Alina bridled at the memory. *As if a Frenchwoman has any right to chide a Russian for haughtiness!*

Abdi laughed gently and raised the window except for one

inch. "Okay?" he inquired and reluctantly she agreed since she couldn't actually feel any wind.

"It doesn't smell the same," he said. "It smells like the earth and the sea."

"The sea? How can it? Kansas is one thousand miles from the sea."

"I smell the sea," he insisted with a laugh.

They entered a small town, drove through it and out again. The name sounded peculiar when he pronounced it. *Strong City?* Ahead, another sign rose up, and she peered at it.

Tall Grass Prairie National Preserve.
One Mile.

She understood the first four words although they did not congeal into a single meaning. Abdi drove slowly as if he were looking for something. There was a bend off the road and here he pulled the taxi in and stopped.

"Picnic!" he announced and pointed again. Around them was a tiny roadside park with a few tables, none of them shaded by trees. Tiny saplings struggled beside two tables, as if someone had considered the need for future shelter. The place was so empty it felt desolate. Who would choose to eat in such an exposed place? All around the small park grass rippled across a treeless landscape, the land rising and falling in gentle swells. Abdi climbed out first and stretched, prodding his family until they all clamored out, and the little girl squealed her pleasure.

"Where are we?" Alina asked.

"I'm not sure, but it's nice, isn't it?"

Khalida appropriated the nearest table and was uncovering and removing the contents of a large food hamper, arranging containers across the picnic table. The little girl helped while the baby, slung across Khalida's back, slept contentedly.

Who could possibly enjoy a place whose name they didn't know? Alina found it unsettling, but Abdi was in no way unsettled and lifted his face into the breeze, holding a bowl for his wife while saying something in Somali to his daughter. Khalida seemed equally unalarmed. For an instant Alina wondered if they were completely daft. Then the spurt of anger vanished, as if it had been only a bird, flying overhead. Its swift departure made her feel strangely light-headed.

"You see?" Abdi let his arms sweep outward, encompassing

the landscape. "Like the ocean. When I was a boy we would go to the ocean, walk along the edge of the water, tossing sticks, tossing stones, finding little crawling animals in shells. The family would come. Watch the sunrise. Sometimes the water would climb up. Other times it rippled and waved like the grass there." He pointed again, outward and beyond, and then shrugged.

"Everything falls apart. No government, no presidents, no help. Little boys like me carrying guns from one hidden man to another, from one small army to another. My father works to keep us together. Mother tries to save us all, but it is no use. We lose one, we lose another, and then we lose Father. Those of us who can run away to Kenya."

Alina held her breath. He had never spoken about himself, and she suddenly wished he would say more. An unfamiliar sorrow swelled inside her. Where was his family now? Had he met Khalida here or in one of those disheartening camps she'd heard about? But how do you ask such a thing, especially when there are two beautiful children and a happy father nearby? Khalida seemed so content organizing the picnic, placing carefully wrapped parcels on the wood table, laughing as she weighted the paper plates and napkins with condiments so the wind would not whisk them away. The baby began to fuss, and she reached one arm around and gently bounced him back to sleep.

A breeze passed over, and Alina removed her scarf. How unlike her, to want to feel the wind brush her face and hair. She couldn't explain this feeling. In this open, uncluttered place the wind belonged, running over the undulating land like an animal.

"Look, Miss Alina. Look at the grass move. Isn't it like your Caspian Sea?"

She gazed out and saw the grass change color as the wind tossed it, just as she had once watched from the embankment as the wind riffled the waves in the bay, changing the color of the water from green to gray to foamy white.

"I like this Kansas!" Abdi announced. "I like its ocean grass."

Khalida was speaking to them, supplicating, her graceful arms escaping the gauzy layers of her blouse, moving in rhythm to the dancing grain. Abdi answered his wife and laughed.

"Eat, Miss Alina! My Khalida says you must eat."

Jonathan Greenhause

Departing from Sengen Jinja

I arrive at Fuji-Yoshida station with all the necessary supplies:
  Warm clothes, water, first-aid kit, raincoat,
& on the way to *Sengen Jinja*, I pick up some *onigiri*,

vinegar-rice stuffed with salmon & tuna wrapped in dried seaweed.
  At the shrine, I eat linguine & white clam-sauce
heated up at the 7-11 & gulp it down with a liter of grapefruit juice.

I ring a bell tied at the top of a frayed rope to invoke the temple's saints,
  clap my hands twice & bow,
my eyes closed for a small eternity before passing beneath

a multitude of *torii* gates made of stone & wood & resembling the *chai*,
  Hebrew letter of life, & several minutes later,
there's a twist in the road that I can either follow or not,

& a picnicking family warns me to remain on the path I'm on,
  but I reject their advice,
taking an uncertain turn & finding myself alone in the forest,

ascending the slopes of Mt. Fuji until the path all but disappears,
  the sound of cars drifting away,
& clouds unleash a lightning storm, sending me cowering

as bolts split the moss-covered labyrinth of trees around me,
  striking to my left & right
& loosening a torrential shower soaking my clothes,

but it's a warm rain, & there's no one else here on this trail,
  the tangled path winding on indefinitely,
& I'm quite sure I've never been this happy in all my life.

Honeymoon

I write this poem on the back of a dog,
both of us in a hammock swinging in this one perfect moment in time,
      the air growing cooler around us
as clouds descend in Ecuador's northern highlands,
swallows slowly circling in the white cloud-covered sky above us,
      only three at first,
then more than two dozen,
& the dog grows restless, stepping twice on my groin,
      but I take it in stride,
this being my honeymoon,
& me having found this peaceful corner in the world
      & knowing that's priceless,

& the dog & I write this poem together,
      me through this pen & paper,
& he through his tranquility,
his vigilant eyes scanning the horizon,
      & we're in a bubble,
in a land out of time & out of view.
I could be anything or anyone right now,
& I turn my head & see my wife on the other side of the platform,
      & she smiles & blows us a kiss,
& a local pick-up game starts up in the distance
with soccer's shouts & the occasional smack of a ball,

& overhead, dozens of swallows still swoop,
one coming so close I hear the whir of its flapping wings,
      & from a nearby pasture
we hear a horse whinny as the air turns chilly,
& the dog cuddles a bit closer, even though it actually got up & left
      about halfway through this poem,
it not being uncommon for my reaction time to be slow,
as if my honeymoon could've taken place years ago
      & the only thing left of it is this.

Tomaž Šalamun

They All

»They all love me here, servants
included. I'll wire you when I
know, Monday morning, after
nine. I'm scared. You stress too

much your ♂'s. I'll take this sweatshirt,
your wedding one. I'll wait for
the next bus. Look, this is San Martin de
Porres, the small black man I was telling you

about. Is my scent nicer than your cat
with white ribbon? I'm not an angel,
I'm a man who wants to experience
that experienced by the one who gave us life.

I'm one of seven children. My father is
three years younger than you. After I leave
you should fall asleep, so your heart doesn't
betray you and you don't lose your wife.«

*Translated from the Slovenian by Michael Thomas Taren
and the author*

Poppy

Cover the people when I step in the area.
Throw on them blankets, tents and powdered milk.
Dig them into the earth, I am a hamster.
Wrap them in a gauze.

Draw crosses on their mouths.
In Biblioteca Lorenziana there's a fire.
Breathe bread and earth and rain,
suffocate your kids with oat bran.

My soul is the dark vigilant agave.
The panther that breaks every cage.
When I march on the stars, my creation,
the white dust creaks under me.

Translated from the Slovenian by Michael Thomas Taren and the author

Tomaž Šalamun

Full Moon

How sweet to meet the childlike soul resting in God!
Eyeballs, lakes and black hair as a beast might have.
The neck you can hold better than a steering wheel
and the laugh the cannibals laughed that I saw in
a movie when I was little. And your scent is real,
Michelangelo's slaves are not as fragrant as you, Francisco.
You shouldn't cry, I cry. Look, even so everything
hangs by a tiny hair. How could I explain this to any reasonable
being and your mom. Do you really think you're not
handsome, ashamed to watch yourself
in the mirror? Stop carrying your comb so primitively
in your pocket. You breathe like bloom and
rower. I like everything you like.
I've never made love listening to Tchaikovsky.

Que te pasa niño!
How do you make so the air crunches and rustles
for us both, and fall asleep like a dew,
so we swim and in the morning you tell me
your dreams and they confirm
you were truly there where I had been.

*Translated from the Slovenian by Michael Thomas Taren
and the author*

PATRICIA FARGNOLI

Biography from Seventy-Four

Once she knew a blind woman
who told her
the dreams of the blind
are full of voices and sound,
the touch of skin on skin—
velvet and satin,
footsteps coming and going,
a hundred bird calls
and the well of darkness.
Her bedroom is small, closed in.
One window, a bureau,
a nightstand piled with books
and a lamp with bad wiring
that flits on and off.
Years ago in a bedroom
with a green lightbulb
she spent many afternoons with a man.
Love is a house afire,
a truck full of apples,
a stream with shining water.
She has one brother,
She has no sisters.
Who are her brothers?
Where are they resting?
Here is a secret:
most days she sleeps
most of the day.
She is not who she was.
Last week, she dreamt
she could still run.
She ran and ran a long way.
She sleeps uneasily now,
waking and turning,
waking and turning.
If she could be anywhere
she'd be in the windjammer
sailing in to Martinique,

the one she remembers
that comes back in dreams,
the sea dark blue and rolling,
that paradise, green mountain
and white sand in the distance.
Don't go back to sleep now.
Love is the sun going down.
She regrets not having been
a better mother.
When she was a child, her mother
sang her to sleep.
The last song always
good night, ladies,
I have to leave you now.
Her fine hair, a flame
wrapped around her head.
Her green eyes.
Suddenly, unannounced,
death came.
Love, a map with no roads,
no boundaries,
wild and full of grace.
Grace: what is given
without being asked,
what makes one able to rise.
The last time she felt joy
so long ago she can't remember.
She is afraid of dying,
of losing those she loves,
of thunder that comes too close,
war and the threat of war.
From these dangers
she protects herself. No,
tries to protect herself—
from the wind of no good.
Her name means *noble.*
she's done the best she could.

Bryce Lillmars

Borgo's

The bartender spears a maraschino cherry
with an umbrella
toothpick from behind the bar, lifting it like a ruby
from its jar of pink formaldehyde to claim
a small island of ice chips
in an aqua-blue beverage with a name I can't remember
but with the allure of an electric violinist
so I ordered it.
I can imagine the allure of naming a drink. I think
it was Blue Lagoon
where a small tribe of women approaches with a bongo
soundtrack and tiki torches
to deliver a ukulele in my lap, or was it
Devil's Masseuse with the maraschino cherry
unzipping its skin over the chaise longue of my tongue?
No, the ice chips brutally
point to Below Zero or Quadruple Lutz on Lake
Jupiter and so this is my third or fourth drink
a Lemon Pinwheel, a Pineapple Mohawk, the rare emerald
maraschino emerging from Disco Swamp.
I've been on African safari, melted on
an asteroid and spun in an Amsterdam underground rave
with the beehives of light to chase me
and I'm still here
without a passport but clearing the haze
to the bathroom, where the gaping mouths of hippos
slosh pink mints the size of hockey pucks
and the music is pulsing my name. My name
has some allure Bryce. Bryce. Bryce.
In a bowl with chopsticks he sounds nice, nice, nice.
The steam lifting from my piss.
A clearing and a waterfall and a shore-hugging cloud of mist
where the tourists throw their towels
and cannonball inside, eloquently twisting
while the water roars and roars.
Somewhere in this jungle, a monkey finds a new grasshopper
dead on the frond of a fern and names it.

A woman pushes out a baby in a bathtub
and wiping the blood from its eyes
she decides
while I touch the four walls of the bathroom
to tame it East. West. North. South
to the street where the sky is so clear you can use your fingers,
your eyelashes, your nose
and point to the stars, burning out
and blinking above you. You can re-name them.
You have that power. The Moon in the Crutch
of a Tree, My Lips, a Ringed Puddle,
the Dangling Cherry of this Endless Unutterable Cup.

James Andrew Smith, *I Held a Jewel in My Fingers*,
oil on panel, 10" x 10"

MATT SCHUMACHER

The World's Only Wooden Skyscraper: Archangelsk, Russia

Ex-
convict
Nicolai
Sutyagin
of Archangelsk,
Russia, constructs
his thirteen-story
wooden skyscraper
largely by himself.
He wants to demonstrate
he's the richest person
in the city. His home's
a hodgepodge of wooden add-ons,
a curiously uneven reverie of shelves.
No elevators service this high rise,
but a hand-carved stairway winds dangerously
to the top. The footing on the upper floors
frightens news reporters.
Fire and notoriety concern the town:
This skyscraper may consist of the longest list
of violated building codes in history.
Sutyagin, arrested for imprisoning a worker
within the house until his work was finished,
enjoys posing shirtless
in front of his imposing house for photos.
In other photographs, the house startles
despite his arrogance: snow curls up
along its monstrous balconies
and mist flirts with its unfinished precipice.

John A. Nieves

A Few Personal Notes on the Recipe for Conjuring Ghosts

Out of habit, I start every meal
with onion, garlic and some
type of pepper. Out of necessity,
I teach them what form to take.
I sweat them, I stew
them, I sear them, I manipulate
the state of their sugars. Later,
I will add the main ingredient,
the item that will name
the meal, but this early work
with the same tools
is what you'll lick
off your lips, is what will ignite,
will flicker on your tongue. Every day,
a new talisman, cooking
like building. I am building
things you will confuse
with stars. You are building
stars. Together, we will hang
them and watch them
sway. Together
we pollute this black
to populate the night. You
who are so much gone
that I build you out of the scents
you left.

GAIL PECK

Postcard of Provence

after van Gogh, 1888

The farmhouse and the fields are the same shade
of wheat, yet the door and windows of the house
are blue. Red flowers grow along a brick wall

that curves away from the stark white pathway,
and to the left a lone figure with his back to us.
My friend who's lost her husband sent this card,

and wrote in handwriting smaller than van Gogh's,
How sad I am. We cannot know this man's life,
what he's walking toward or away from, his occupation,

only that a ghostly sky meets a field of lavender,
that one tree has bloomed purple behind haystacks.
He could be a widower, carrying his loneliness

with every step, no one to hear *I'm home*, vases empty,
and work still to be done—threshing of wheat,
shaking the olive trees until they let go their bitter fruit.

From the collection of the Editor, photograph

Hay

(Not to be confused with straw)

Ryegrass, timothy, brome, fescue, Bermuda grass, orchard grass, alfalfa, clover, oat, barley, wheat, switch grass, leechweed, sinner's forbs, bleeder's fetch, thirst-rooted ruminant.

The riots of hay are organized into square or round bales, the ones you drove by in the back seat as a teenager as your parents' questions suffocated you. The bales are sprayed with salt or wrapped in light plastic, with one area left open to the air. Hay is like you in that it must be allowed to breathe.

Illnesses related to hay:

Botulism:

In the bale of rolled hay lies a dead snake or a mouse, and as it sits its death turns into a core of black tar that infests the rest and makes toxic hay. A human exposed to this hay is put on a mechanical respirator. This is like when you escaped your parents' house and walked the dark neighborhood, infuriating in its utter stillness, under the equally fixed stars. The streetlights changed colors uselessly over the deserted streets. Tomorrow would come and you would have to choose another mask. You turned up your headphones until a dead man's roar made your teeth rattle. Because sometimes you need someone to breathe for you.

Hay belly:

A horse is fed bad hay and its hindgut distends due to the influx of empty calories fermenting in that wet chamber. It is essentially like eating ash. The horse can be gaunt in every other part of its body, ribs exposed, but its belly will hang low, an equine contradiction of excess and sickness. As in the year you wore Xs on your hands and did not drink or smoke like the others and volunteered for people you were terrified of and smiled until it was hard to pull the pins that held up your face when at last you reached the sweet black ocean of your room.

Black Bale:

This is when, of a night, all of a farmer's bales turn black. The ombudsman of hay will be mystified. Much as you were when you called your mother a name you never thought you could. You were more shorn of breath than she was. You spent the night swearing *never*, withdrawing deeper inside of yourself, your chest full of black hay.

Hay dust, the brittle convulsive air that trails a harvest, is one of the most flammable materials known to man. If sparked, the atmosphere itself can catch fire, causing sheets of flame to climb the detritus up to the treeline, and even higher into the register of crows. If you do not cover your mouth, the flames can leap into your lungs, making the cells of your body, for a few seconds, nourished by fire. This is like nothing you have known, except how you felt when you drove out into the country after rubbing a wound into your arm with a protractor, the heat of it keeping your mind conscious of your senses: wind, pain, thick tang of culled grain in your nose, the pressure on your sternum like a huge Bible lying across you. If only your mind could be as orderly as those fields, and when it was gnarled, it could be threshed clean and resown. You could see your life reduced to its framework, like seeing from above that the landscape was made up only of structures of hay. A world both endless and knowable. You could see that it was possible to make of your mind a small field of flame.

Kitty Jospé

Postcards

Dear one,
Here no midnight cicadas call—
only water slap on the cluttered catch of boats.
During the day artists rain lavender paint
on cupola, campanile
but I look at three black-eyed windows
that stare like pinned ghosts in the ochre
washing the facade. — Claudette

        Ma Chère Claudette,
        Each morning, could you make yourself up,
        shake awake reasons for friendship, and
        make a self someone else can relate to?
        It's dreary staring at these giant wheels of hay,
        staking naked shadows in the field.
        They roll you from my summer memory to
        sun-splattered shivers of white.
        I imagine you as one of my black figures
        wiggling an umbrella against the snow
        under the thumbprint sun. — Claude

Dear One,
It is long after sunrise,
and flames are working into the arches.
I've just read your card for the 100th time,
feeling like the bone-pillars climbing the blue wall
of sky, veins all a-tremble. — Claudette

        Ma Chère Claudette,
        Do not worry. The sadness of happiness
        is not asking anything to change.
        Shadows watch the play of the sun on stones:
        they don't ask for a turn in the garden. — Claude

Mon cher Claude,
The lilt of sail is in love, tips
as if for the first time, just enough ready

Kitty Jospé

       to be unfurled
       but the water's heartline falls
       into zig-zagged rips
       ship after ship
       sparring. —Claudette

The postcards are reproductions of paintings by Claude Monet. In stanza order, *Grand Canal Venice, Haystack in Winter, Rouen Cathedral, Full Sunlight, Japanese Garden, Ships in a Harbor.*

From the collection of the Managing Editor, photograph

Overheard in my Neighborhood

Morning shadows the cracked sidewalk
and Vivienne. She yells in creole
give me back the umbrella
rain is spitting on the baby
and something about ten dollars
and how he's a good-for-nothing
notching each hour with cigarette smoke—
then stomps into her house tattered shut with shades.
She has left the stroller with the baby by the door
of the duplex she shares with other refugees from the Congo.

Vivaldie is on the porch, pushing at her belly.
It's swollen with badly-healed knife wounds and an abortion.
She says she can't stop
feeling her flesh, and the memory
of the men who raped her. You believe her,
watching her eyes roll as if inside her mind,
to her burning village, hell-flamed night
charred with the sound track
of machine guns and madness.

The baby starts mewling. Vivaldie runs to cradle it,
whispers *God is Good*
the only English she's learned
to ask for peace and safety.

Ihab Hassan

Tahrir

Kateb, my name, means writer in Arabic. But I am not a writer; I am a widower, dabbling in memories, and I have forgotten my native speech. Once I served as foreign correspondent for papers in the Bay Area. Now I savor my resignation, tell stories about my granddaughter, Leila, and miss my dearest Anne.

Egypt, which I departed long ago, has recently swamped the news: protests, heady change, the riptide of uncertainties. Yet all I can hear is a distant dirge: dreams sputtering like a burned wick, harsh melodies of grief, and the cries of Leila in her last agony. Of small hopes and vast miseries the world is made—but that's not what the history books say. Nor can history speak of my timeless moment in the lees of Sinai.

❊ ❊ ❊

Leila doted on her Egyptian heritage—at her age, she could hardly have claimed a personal past. Her American mother had died of pancreatic cancer when the child was only ten; her father— that's my son, Walid—never remarried, keeping his beaked nose buried in some hush-hush work at a GE lab in Schenectady. It was her maternal Aunt Helen who brought up Leila, smiling on her niece's breakneck ways. I did the best I could from the distance of Boston Common and could not decide whether my granddaughter took after her mother, russet curls fringing her face, or after her grand-uncle, Moktar. The family called him mad but he was inspired.

Leila—olive skin and unflinching olive eyes—wanted to know about genealogies and guiding stars. I tried to persuade her that tribal blood is thinner than the waters of life. She said: "Tell me about Egypt, Grandpa. Tell me why you left." Her look was tender and wild. I gave her rumors of my past, truancies of time. She scribbled notes with a red-lacquered pen—tight, looping hand—her auburn hair raveling down. "Tell me about your departure," she pleaded, tossing her hair aside. I said to myself: this girl would leave a full fridge, a soft bed, and white lace curtains to join the *peshmerga* in the fastness of the Caucasus. Sure enough, Leila decided she must visit tombs and temples of her forebears.

But that's not all: unbeknown to me, Leila disturbed the sense of my Egyptian past. Whenever I spoke to her—and for days afterwards—I confused tenses and pronouns.

※ ※ ※

If his last year in Egypt is critical—a crux, perhaps, of modern history—the period remains for Kateb fogged by personal obsessions and rumors of war. For his parents, names like Tobruk and El Alamein seem vaguely ominous. Ominous of what? Moktar shouts—in a spell of clarity, shortly before his suicide—as he paces the family living room: Sure, the Allies blench at the mere thought of the Desert Fox rampaging toward the Suez Canal and the oil fields of Arabia.

Rolling his eyes, he looks at Kateb and laughs:

Imagine the Afrika Korps lounging by the reflecting pool of the Taj Mahal! But what is it to any of us?

Kateb's parents say nothing; they know Moktar is right if often perverse. To them, the war is just a forlorn Lewis gun pointing idly at the sky from the rooftop of their stately villa near Kubri el Ingleez (renamed El Gal'a, or Evacuation Bridge, after the English left).

While other Egyptians finger their beads, count their piasters, and watch Tommies, Diggers, and GIs board their transport ships, young Kateb prepares for his own departure. Behind him are the days of studying maps (stained with the pale pink of the British Empire), making fussy lists (resolutions of self-improvement), or cramming from law books as he awaits his appointment to some consulate in America. His ordeals are now of a different kind: He must secure his passage—the Allies' ships are loaded to the Plimsoll Line—and he must pass an exacting medical examination to qualify for his visa. The doctors peer, pound, and prod, and order his first pair of glasses.

One morning, his father calls him to his study with the large roll-down desk and built-in bookcases, all colors there in rich shades of brown.

Mabrouk! Twice Mabrouk! First, on the medical report.

Thank you, Papa.

Second, on your new post. The Ministry just called. You're going to San Francisco.

Kateb hears a sharp intake of breath, his own.

His mother walks in, wearing her apricot peignoir, black bangs across her brow. She appears casual but self-absorbed. His father glances at her furtively then scratches his chin:

A pity you already need spectacles.

Kateb hears the covert reproach and thinks: At least I've escaped the fate of those naked, country urchins, bellies swollen with dysentery, eyes blackened with swarming flies. His mother's insidious perfume begins to fill the study, blending into the smell of leather, tobacco, and books. In her velvety voice, she says:

Chéri, they will make you look older, the glasses. But never mind, those long-legged American girls will fall for you.

She pretends to pout her Clara Bow lips:

Anyway, you'll soon forget us all.

Already the young diplomat, he says soothingly:

I'll be all right, Maman. And I'm not forgetting anyone here.

But he has already started to forget; he has always felt alien in Egypt. Even beggars call him khawaga, *Mr. Foreigner, as they cry baksheesh, baksheesh! on Cairo streets.*

❈ ❈ ❈

In Boston, I had a dark, roomy flat on Exeter Street, overlooking a sliver of the Charles, with an improvised conservatory in a corner and potted ferns under the glass roof. It was my corner of light. When Leila visited me, she liked to sit with me there, drinking thick Turkish coffee out of small cups. Ignoring the Charles River, she fondled the brass coffee pot resting on arabesque tiles—coffee set and tiles, her gift to me—and talked. Her mind darted like blue electric sparks. "Tell me about Egypt," she said, "what it is really, really like." And I would always start by answering, "Oh, but I left so long ago." I knew I couldn't speak to her of that moment, pure transparency.

A few weeks before her departure for Egypt, Leila came visiting again. I thought I could dissuade her from taking that tour. (Imagine a young woman, lovely to behold, an *efrangiya* at that, wandering about Cairo, poking about in souks, mosques, and the back alleys of Khan el Khalili, all on her own.) But how could I dissuade her? The day she arrived, we had barely kissed cheeks and closed the front door when she took one long, slanting look at me and said:

"Grandpa, here's the deal. I'll consider your advice. But no preaching, *please*."

Walid had little influence with her, absorbed as he was in his secret distractions, his work for the Pentagon. (Father and daughter had long ago signed a friendly, absent-minded truce.) As for Helen, I think she covertly approved willfulness in her niece, missing a touch of vividness, a hint of mischief, in her own small-town life. And so I bided my time, watching for a flicker in Leila's will, a shadow of hesitation, while regaling her with anecdotes of Egypt. It was like throwing small bits of meat to appease ravening wolves.

During her week-long stay with me, Leila scoured the Boston Public Library, the Museum of Fine Arts, and the Athenaeum for information about Egypt. She could tell you anything about the Nilometer at Elephantine, the radiography of mummies, Cleopatra's adder, the horsemen of Amr Ibn el Aas, and the latest exploit of the Mamur Zapt. I nodded and smiled but thought to myself: Can knowledge sate the torturer's eye or stay the rapist's hand? Can origins confer wisdom and roots answer a child's cry for love?

One day, when she had been rummaging into my Egyptian life, I looked coldly at Leila over my demitasse, wondering why she lacked any curiosity about people closer to home: her father, say, or her grandmother, my own Anne. Stop, I admonished myself, stop, Leila's needs are her own—what if she needs to reach into the deep past? What are memories, anyway, but makeshift words and dispiriting blanks?

Of all people, I should have known that. When I tried to recall high moments in Egypt, moments that brought existence to a quivering pitch or slammed the spirit hard against the ribs—recall events that would embed themselves forever in a person's heart—I blanked out, as if my vantage, once lofty and sweeping with the recklessness of youth, had sunk into a tarn. Ah, but there was that moment in Sinai, dimmed by the irrelevancies of recall.

❊ ❊ ❊

The tall villa is in gloom. The ceiling fans whir, their arms ceaselessly turning, moving the air without freshening the place; the servants walk on tiptoes. Kateb's parents go from room to room, slightly bemused, as if they had misplaced some object, a watch, a ring, the front door keys. As she passes him on the stair, on her way to her boudoir, his mother says:

Alors, Kateb, you're off to America, are you? Any day now, your father says. Beware those foreign girls.

Kateb thinks of hugging her but the gesture seems awkward on the canted stairs:

Oh, but we'll meet in Europe, Maman. At one of those spas you and Papa love. Vichy or Karlsbad.

She looks at him and her dark eyes brim with reproach. Kateb finds nothing to say. He smiles wistfully and passes by.

It is an ageless story, this story of families about to sunder. Add here: Kateb's tacit repudiation of a mother tongue. But which tongue? Arabic, French, English, or some ur-sounds — words behind words — that no one can utter? Kateb cannot hear his own accent in all the languages he speaks.

❊ ❊ ❊

"Your accent is real cool, Grandpa," Leila said.

We were breakfasting in the conservatory, Leila and I. Sleet and grime splotched the glass. I recalled how Anne used to tease me about my taste for foggy beaches — I am an enterprising swimmer. "Anything but the heat and clarity of Egypt?" she would say with a glint in her violet eyes, and I would reply: "I like the clarity of deserts well enough, Anne." For ten seconds, she would give me her Giaconda quarter-smile, then squeeze my hand before walking away, imprinting the moment with her indelible grace.

Leila, though, had the ferocity of youth on her side:

"I'm flying to Cairo in a few days, Grandpa, and you still haven't told me why you discourage my going to Egypt. Or why you left."

"Look, Leila, I worked as a foreign correspondent for many years after I left the consular service. I know something about the world and I don't have a good feeling about this trip."

She raised an ironic eyebrow that nearly stopped my speech.

"People are restless now," I continued evasively. "The despots have built their palaces on sand. Soon the hot Khamsin wind will blow everything away."

"This is *January*, Grandpa, not April or March. The Khamsin doesn't blow in winter."

She paused to take a greedy bite of her croissant, small teeth glistening, and her look became sly:

"Anyway, I'm taking my shots and plenty of aspirin for

the Khamsin."

"Shots against poverty, corruption, tyranny? Aspirin?"

I sounded graveled and peevish; I didn't like the way I sounded:

"Just what do you want me to say, Leila? I'm not the only one to have left his native plot. The earth is scarred with diasporas now."

She looked at me, eyes dark jade, her expression winsome even in defiance. Then she stood up, deftly collected the breakfast dishes, and walked out of the conservatory. A bit later, I heard her opening drawers in the spare bedroom. Dirty rivulets snaked across the panes as I wondered how I could appease Leila's craving. I felt betrayed by ignorance of my own life—by my perverse reticence, too. Just then, Leila came in with her hands behind her back:

"Grandpa, I splurged. Yesterday, I bought designer sunglasses."

She put them on and canted her head this way and that:

"How do you like them?"

I was shocked: Leila was transformed, half Lolita, half Audrey Hepburn, Leila still.

"Well?" She insisted, showing her profile. "Would the sungod Ra approve?"

"They're quite alluring."

She took me by the hand and pulled me out of my chair:

"Come. And quit worrying about me. I just want to know something about my name. Mom and Dad hardly talked about it."

We walked together to the kitchen and started to wash the dishes, talking about small things as the water splashed.

* * *

A week before he will hang himself from an attic rafter by the belt of his robe, Moktar says to Kateb:

You want to go to America, don't you? Well, keep going...

They are strolling in the villa's garden while Kateb's parents sit on the veranda, sipping lemonade and watching them walk among jasmine bushes and orange trees. Waving to his parents from a distance, Kateb says breathlessly:

Uncle Moktar, in a few weeks I'll be in Port Said. I have a berth on a cargo. They call it a Liberty Ship. That's all I know.

Moktar plucks a jasmine, puts it to his nose, then restores it carefully to its stem. They take a few turns in silence. They will never see each other again.

❉ ❉ ❉

Two days before boarding the Abraham Lincoln, *Kateb has a strange impulse: though he practices no religion, he feels the need to make a parting gesture, a votive offering to Egypt. And he feels the need to purify himself. Why not a long swim in the Mediterranean, which he must cross anyway?*

Across the Suez Canal lies a pristine, unprotected shoreline, its beaches deserted, scattered strips of sand between the blue-green sea and red rocks of Sinai. Carrying only a light beach bag, Kateb rides the ferry to Port Fuad, then walks beyond the last bungalows of the town. He finds a tiny bay, cradled by headlands of sandstone, veined with chalcedony. The bay slopes gently toward deeper waters, indigo where kelp and seaweed float.

For an instant, Kateb thinks of sharks, jellyfish, undertows. But he sees no black dorsal fin slicing the surface, no shoals of jellyfish drifting like small, translucent clouds. As for currents, well…the low surf sparkles like liquid quartz, tumbling, disappearing in the sand. Kateb sheds all his clothes, folds and piles them on a towel, and wades to his waist in the water. He flexes his legs, jackknifes high into the air, and dives.

He does not think, just swims a steady crawl, rolling slightly, and keeps swimming till he can hardly discern the shore. Then he swims still farther out, feeling no hint of fear or fatigue. For him, it is a moment of pure transparency, of lightness and grace, as if he had wholly shed his body, or rather, as if his consciousness, suffusing every cell, had itself become naked flesh. Nothing in the sky or sea seems alien to him, nothing extraneous or strange. He has no desire to do anything, go anywhere; he does not say to himself, this is freedom.

The moment—a second? a minute?—ends abruptly. His arms, his shoulders and head now cast a shadow on the water; his muscles tighten; goosepimples appear on his skin. He circles with an effort against the tide and with a sliding breaststroke makes for the shore. He swims till all his muscles ache. At last, he crawls out on land, hands and knees, feeling his chest heave, hot air rushing into his lungs. On his back, Kateb rubs his eyes hard, purple sparks blazing under his lids.

After a while, he sits up, still gulping for air. Where, where has it gone? He searches for something he has lost out at sea, there, out there, in the deep.

❉ ❉ ❉

History is brisk and indifferent to those who drop through its cracks. On a drizzling January afternoon, the skies sullen and low, I rode with Leila in a taxi to Logan Airport. I felt listless but her mood was high. In Tunisia, revolt had blazed and rulers had gone up in malodorous smoke; embers flew across the Middle East. I didn't have to say to my granddaughter, "I told you so." She was excited and knew what she knew. Her excitement glowed about her like a corona as I huddled beside her in my thick overcoat. All the way through the Callahan Tunnel and past Satori Stadium, she chattered. We said goodbye at Security. Before she could give me a hug fit to crack my bones, I said:

"No postcards. But text me. No jargon, please."

She caught the reference to her earlier phrase, "no preaching, please," and poked me in the arm. We left it at that.

On my way back, I imagined Leila in wartime Cairo, seven decades earlier, suddenly hearing an air-raid siren and, rushing up to the roof of our house in bare feet, scanning the starry skies to rip out their mystery. Nothing daunted that girl—but where would her freedom lead?

❊ ❊ ❊

The events at Tahrir Square ravished the media. At first, I thought: this is a whizz-bang that will never explode. Then I thought, by God, Egyptians are reclaiming their country. The text messages from Leila, before they snuffed out the Internet, helped to clue me in: **Awesome . . . it really rocks . . . come, hear the music play . . . bawdy, baladi, and cool . . . the Rhino's stampeding outa the gate . . . .** That's how she texted until darkness fell on Leila, whose name means night.

At the time, I knew nothing of her grievous hour. I sat in the conservatory sipping coffee, pretending that Leila was out, cramming at some Boston library; or else I followed the news on TV, gazing at the screen with wonder and disbelief. I watched millions of Masri—that's what Egyptians still call themselves—take to the streets in civic epiphanies. I learned how they protected their ancient heritage, improvised clinics, canteens, festivals, and then cleaned up their messes before they left. Despite myself, I felt stirrings of something I refused to call pride—call it admiration, I said to myself, call it respect, but why would I call it pride? And what, after all this? Still, it was "awesome," this feeling for Masr, a name that could send a whole country howling after freedom.

Quixotically, I went to my laptop and Foxfired the word Masr: Pharaonic Hwt-ka-Ptah, mispronounced by Greeks as Aigyptos, renamed by Arabs as Masr, which just means country. Country or *balad*? A plot of earth, a strip of water, a crust of rock, wobbling and careening through space. In Masr, eighty million saw their first light and would probably die. But when or where does anyone of us become light? Sitting before the cretinous TV screen, I suddenly recalled my unbounded moment in the bay. Through all the intervening years, I could never fit that moment to a word or place.

※ ※ ※

Two weeks passed: no text or tweet from Leila, no postcard. Then Helen called, her voice trilling with agony:

"No news from Leila. Walid has just boarded a military transport to Cairo. He knows someone in the Pentagon. Just told me to call you and wait. It's all very well for him to say wait."

"He's right, Helen. There's nothing you or I can do. Just now, the place is bedlam. Finding a girl there with a name like Leila . . ."

I don't want to hear this.

She hung up. I consoled myself: Walid, who had also spurned his past, would take personal charge and his connections might finally pay off. But in times like this, I always think of Anne. (We were married for forty-four years before she died in her sleep, the trace of a smile on her face.) I think of her because no one has ever come closer to me in flesh or soul. But I also think of her because acute loss evokes for me a fantasy that I always recall with shame.

The scene is always a desert, far from the living swath of the Nile—silt, palms, cotton fields, rice paddies—far from platted roads and swarming towns. The sands curve and wave like a yellow sea. I am lost and the wind instantly erases my tracks. But I know that Anne is looking for me, sometimes in a low-flying plane, sometimes on a swaying dromedary. I hear the distant drone of the plane or see the silhouette of the animal against the dunes. And my irresistible urge is to burrow deep into a sandbank, letting my rescuer pass. When I wake up from that reverie, I feel relieved and indescribably forlorn.

Once, when I shared this fantasy with Anne, she just turned her face to the wall.

❊ ❊ ❊

In Cairo, Walid encounters everywhere exhilaration and chaos. The staff at the American Embassy proceeds catch-as-catch-can, sifting through bushels of rumors about missing tourists. Most leads are dead ends. Leila's tour company reports no "sighting" of her—odd word, Walid thinks—after 28 January, the Friday of Rage. A young vendor, whose uncle works at the Consulate, says he sold an efrangiya *with Leila's description a pair of red leather slippers—that was after thugs on camels had rampaged through the Square—but he doesn't know the girl's name. By leaflet and word of mouth, Walid posts a reward of a thousand Egyptian pounds for reliable information concerning his daughter.*

Cranks and con men call; Walid dismisses them with a few words of his learned-in-Boston Arabic and a scowl on his unlined brow. Early one morning, though, a student at the American University reaches him at the Semiramis Intercontinental, a stone's throw from Tahrir Square. Through his jet-lagged sleep, he catches her name, Soraya; but she won't say more. Within the hour, they meet in the hotel lobby and Walid leads her to a quiet corner with rattan chairs under house-grown palms. The girl is small and wiry—quick eyes, perky nose, rapid speech—dressed in a long, taupe frock, a rainbow scarf tied neatly to conceal her hair. She speaks fluent, mildly accented English.

It appears that Soraya has spent a "week or so" with Leila at the Square, sleeping in the same tarpaulin "freedom motel." They talked about everything, including her family in America. But she has not seen her ochty, *her sister Leila, since the 11th of February, when The Dog stepped down. Walid remains skeptical. He asks what family names Leila mentioned. Soraya tells him. He asks:*

What else did you talk about?

Soraya's penciled eyebrows tighten:

Everything. We talked about everything while her family slept in their clean American beds. But I don't know where she went.

Walid remains impassive, leaning slightly, unthreateningly, toward the girl:

Did anyone bother her, follow her around?

Soraya glares at Walid and her face becomes a small thundercloud. He continues without ceasing to look her steadily in the eye:

Soraya, I'm trying to find my daughter. Please forget the cultural politics now.

Still bristling, she answers:

There were other foreign women among us. Reporters.

She pauses and the thundercloud lifts slowly from her face:

Anyway, Leila could take care of herself. She wore a plastic bucket for a helmet and soaked her scarf in Coca-Cola. She could man the concertina-wire barricades while wearing those ridiculous sunglasses. She loaned her iPhone to some of our organizers.

At the last sentence, Walid represses a groan. He asks matter-of-factly:

Soaked her scarf?

We soaked scarves, kerchiefs, rags against tear gas.

Soraya suddenly clouds over again:

Actually, there was a tall man, sort of tough-looking. No beard, though. He eyed her from a distance. We thought he might be from the Special Police. He didn't touch her but seemed fascinated by her glasses.

She stops suddenly and shrugs:

Maybe things will change for women after Tahrir. We know the way to the Square now.

Walid nods, his leaden heart near his feet. Where will he go now? Not to the police. What will he tell his father or his sister-in-law? Soraya can feel his misery; his face remains a mask of desolation with a rictus for mouth:

Anyway, I don't want your money. I don't know where your daughter went.

Walid leans over, opens forcibly the girl's purse, and stuffs the money in it. The following day, the American Consul himself phones Walid at his hotel. Walid already knows.

※ ※ ※

I waited for my son at Logan Airport. His plane was two hours late. When he emerged at last from the crowd—bedraggled yet still self-possessed—I embraced him as I had not done in years. Taking Walid by the arm as we waited at the luggage carousel, I said:

"Did you know that you arrived at the same gate?"

He understood; he would think it logical anyway. But a slight tic began to play on his face, as if struggling to conceal something—something indecent and horrendous—from public view. He looked at the slow-moving bags, nearly all black, piled helter-skelter on the shuddering belt, and with lowered head, whispered:

"They found her in the Nile, Father. A few miles from Tahrir Square. She was in very bad shape. Do you understand, in very bad shape . . ."

I hugged him again before he or I could collapse, hugged him a long time, till I felt calm enough to step back into the world.

Joyce Smith, photograph

JAMES K. ZIMMERMAN

The Dream About the Plane

going down in a cornfield near Paducah
or a lake around Odessa Texas or Ukraine
or a monastery in Daramsala or maybe
Tanzania in flames or probably
not since we sat in comfort in an aisle
seat near the wing that was still there

or at a breezy coffee shop in the Food
Court at the Mall of America watching
the nose slowly glide to earth and settle
peacefully in a garden of lilacs and butter-
fly bushes and coconut palms and
I was pruning the lilacs as we nosed in
and slid to a stop in the sugar cane or
the waters of Lake Titicaca or maybe yes
it was the Atlantic near Reykjavik or

but the water was calm like an Aztec
cornfield until I started to notice it
rocking silently in my ears and thought
maybe I'd get sick or be dead so I opened
the window and asked are we in water

and meanwhile back at the atrium in
the Food Court or the royal palace we
were all surprised to be sole survivors
in the lilac-laden wreckage and soul
survivors metempsychosed into the bodies
of eagles or eared seals or Chevy Impalas
or maybe Boeing 747s or Piper Cubs
or lions on the African savanna

and so we sipped our green corn tea or
Kenyan latte or Bombay gin in the atrium
and the ventricles pulsing again and I
asked are we in water and the lilacs
nodded yes or maybe you were now
the lilacs nodding yes

William Winfield Wright

The View from Space

The Great Wall? A failure
at least as far as walls go. We can just go around,

and half the people anything is designed
to keep out are always already there.

The Pyramids? Ditto,
lovely in the war against algebra

but nonstarters in making mummies walk
or protecting your stuff for the future.

The Great Lakes? We didn't build them,
they need salt, and they leave Chicago where Chicago is.

There's an exact model of your DNA
inside each of my drunk and maudlin cells

but it looks like everyone else's
and even with your eyes and a mirror

I can't see it.
The view from space, however, is perfect,

everything small and close to the water,
everyone missing and safe,

everywhere lonely and important.

Close to the Water

I like how everyone's an expert.
If you hit the water at 200 mph
it's like hitting a brick wall.
How do you know that?
And by that logic if we lean
gently against that brick wall
is that like wading,
and if we learn to lie softly
on top of the bricks
is that a kind of floating?

I'd like to do that, touch down,
touch down onto the tarmac
like it's water,
walk on the ground like it's ocean.
Let's do that. Let's do that
individually or in whole big groups.

Emily Benson

The Problem with Paradise

From Key Largo, we drive down the great white spine
of the Overseas Highway, the ocean a gelatinous expanse
of turquoise, too improbable to be real,
lucid and orderly as an in-ground swimming pool.

Even the pelicans seem disappointed
their long faces exhausted by so many graceless landings
as they fumble through the air with the disastrous flair
of malfunctioning aircrafts.

Happiness is far more elusive than the easy paradise
promised by couples on honeymoon brochures;
it comes in bursts and flashes, like the nervous dash
of a neon green lizard across a slumbering gray rock

or a two-day train ride back to New York, with nothing but stale bread
and wine to sustain us, necks sore from sleeping in our seats
when I awake to find your black-fabric jacket
draped over my curled form like a cavernous tent of sleep

the vague reminder of your cologne
burrowed deep in the collar
the long tunnels of its sleeves
still lit with fleeting dreams.

The Day's Catch

On the neighbor's dock, a ghost-white bucket lingers
at the far end, the day's catch left to putrefy
in deadening heat. When I peer inside,
blue crabs sit submerged in warm water,
silent, motionless as a stack of plates.

Foolish with hope, I attempt to set them free
into the shallow marsh beneath the suck and release
of the tide. But when I empty out the bucket, the crabs
tumble to the water with sorrowful weight, the tumultuous
stiffness of bodies to a mass grave.

Upside down, their bellies, pillowed with white meat,
glimmer like a heap of diaphanous trash. Alongside them,
beneath the cool water, the living scamper in their sideways ballet.
blue needle-nosed pincers flung open for rough play, claws lit
with the fire of existence, a sudden match-tip redness.

Leslie Ringold, photograph

Stan Zumbiel

Eddie Autumn and His Trio

His father drinking, my friend
needs to escape. I have my father's car.
It is newly dark and we blow smoke
out the wing windows and listen to
"The Girl from Ipanema."
He uses the vinyl seat as a snare
and keeps the slow beat of "On
Broadway" and we sing together
the chorus,

waiting for small
planes to land at Maidu Field, their
lights pulsing red and green. No
one knows where we are.

We burn rubber to DJ's to sip banana
shakes among empty stools
and tables. It's dead. We match
quarters, I call even, lose, and slip my coin
into the cigarette machine.

Four men come in lost, finding this

joint far off the main
drag—eight
o'clock at night—Eddie Autumn and his
Trio—sport coats and skinny
ties, pants tight and shiny shoes
with pointed toes—a gig in
Tahoe—Harrah's.

They push through the door
and join us in the harsh
fluorescent pool,
six anonymous heads surrounded by an unlit
town.

The men joke with us
and exhale, Eddie through a straw says, "It waxes
the shit out of you."
The drummer, hunched with high shoulders
cigarette hanging loose from his lip,
beats a rhythm on the Formica and scat
sings what I now know is Billie Holliday's
"Trav'lin' Light."

Burgers finished, Eddie and his boys,
like specters, get in their two-door Chevy

coupe and make toward the highway
again. At

the Feather River we shine headlights into parked
cars—heads pop up from the back seats. We
flick cigarette butts into the water, find
flat stones to skip across the moonlit shallows. Shadows
slip between packed gravel as
if to pry them loose and tumble
them down the sides of the
piles of dredge tailings.
Footfall on loose rubble
echoes the crunch
all unnoticed, devoured
by darkness and the lapse of
memory.
We ride our bikes for hours
through orchards and housing
developments pretending we're
running away from home, riding
the flat roads of the Midwest
searching for what
might meet us,
might be at risk for discovery.

We drop into the darkness and
spot a doe, blood running from her mouth,
legs splayed

where she slid
down the gravel.

We stand silent,
her empty eyes look back at us. I wish I had words for
prayer, but I light
another cigarette and we return to the car. Blackness

receives her.

He enters his midnight
house, father quiet and sleeping it off, mother
asleep too, having said her prayers.

Alone now

I return to a quiet dark suburban ranch
house, my world
distilled to the flat
tastelessness of a full pack of
cigarettes smoked. I

want to spit as I put my dad's
wagon into park. My
parents too sleep in separate
silences.

It was this night I thought of

when he came to me
and we lay next to one another in
silence and confusion
fearful of embrace;

when he burned beach fires
trying to move
some unnamed god to reveal
answers that we couldn't find that night
or in the nights since;

when six years later he called
in the middle of the night not
remembering where he was
in the conversation, repeating
himself and playing the sound
track for *Easy Rider* over and
over saying "listen to this" and
"listen to this." Wife asleep
and not listening.

I look into the
cloudless, midnight sky, and envision
other worlds spinning closely to our own. I

could step off ours and onto
another like stepping from the hard
deck of the boardwalk to a moving
merry-go-round, the breathy calliope
echoing marches and circus

songs. I cannot imagine
what bubbles to the surface,
what takes me back
to the river to stand on dredge
tailings exultant,
facing the night as if all
scripture led to only one

end. I don't sleep. Eddie Autumn
plays something on an upright
so far away I can't hear it, and his sax
player puts down a solo
just out of reach.

Suze Baron

Lucienne

I was sittin
with Papa
on the front porch

all of a sudden
he jumped up
    and yelled

        Don't you
        come
          in here

        out out out
        tha-a-way
        tha-a-way

his fingers
pointed to
ward the streets

I looked
  saw nobody
  saw nobody

only later
Madeleine's
fiancé Michel

took sick
he'd sit
head down

won't sleep
won't speak
won't eat

They say
he had
    a mistress

didn't want
him to
marry

sent a ghost
to get
    his girl

Papa saw
the ghost
drove him

away
The ghost
without

a host
got at
    Michel

The mistress
    came
        a-runnin

She came
    a-runnin
        too late.

Nadine Sabra Meyer

The Lace-Maker's Bloom

Lace muffles the warming trays, so when her children
come to her, faces cross, hair ratted by schoolyard
bullying, she can fill them with bacon drippings, potatoes
flavored with lard, chunks of warm cheese.
The doorknocker, too, she's muffled in lace, an announcement —
to anyone who comes to the splintering door — of the birth,
this child milk-heavy in her dress or rocking, as she is now,
by her foot. Oh, the industrious hour of near solitude, her foot working
the treadle of the cradle, her mind cooling blank but for the blue square
of the lace-maker's pillow, the hundred bobbins,
the linen thread's torque and tighten! How she loves the cell
of quietude, this caesura in which no infant shrieks, no child pulls
hard on the apron of her mind, and the whole universe is paused for
there is no husband here in this moment to rave the seams of her chest
open, only this careful darning-up, loop, twist, cross, over someone else's
pattern, and it's lovely, it's lovely, it's lovely! This cauliflower lace collar
can turn her daughter's coarse dress fine. And how it sells
on the market; they all want it, what she can do up in an hour's
peace, the threads liquid in her fingers, drips of chartreuse, inky
blood-red and the many, many humors of blue. Let the churchmen
call it trivial, vanity, the lace which decorates frock fronts and dresser tops,
the oh-so-easily-torn veil of pillowcase. She calls it beauty, and isn't
that what beauty is, that which conceals and reveals in patterns spun
like bloom: a net the finer spun, the more easily rent. It's nun's work, too,
she'd like to tell them, and she knows it, the nun's meditation,
the body lax but for the fingers' focus, the fine singing
of her fingers through a web, chrysanthemum, chrysanthemum.

Jose Trejo-Maya

Chilam Balam

1. I was born in seconds
   the first hero twin not
   Hunter or *Jaguar Deer*,
   I mean the title see Jaguar Priest.
   Next to rivers and wind sweep.

2. I was born aura presence
   to speak what you can't.
   Then freeze blue terrain,
   remains between
   mountainside and jade-eyes

3. I was born on the tenth
   day of the twenty-day
   cycle *Atlacahualo*:
   What's brought by the waters.

4. I was born to speak eloquent
   and sharp edges
   turn to laughter.

5. I was born were life's
   worth a dollar's toss
   freeze bone marrow.

6. I was born in the 365-day cycle
   called *Chicome Tecpatl*:
   otherwise obsidian/flint night
   hold this teardrop.

7. I was born in between a culture
   clash, two braids in the locks;
   there's three stripes on the right
   cheek to cut through.

   What you despise.

LaTanya McQueen

On the Terra Roxa Earth We Saw Stars

My brother Felix is charging tourists to see the streets of the favela. For 30 reis he says he'll show them the authentic favela experience, one only someone like him can provide. Marcos and I are walking home when he meets up with us to talk about his plan.

"30 reis? What do you do that someone would pay that much?" Marcos asks.

"I show them around. I make up stories. They drink it up like the sugary fresco drinks they buy at the stands. You should see their faces."

"For 30 reis? What made you come up with that number?"

"I asked around. Look, I'm not the only one doing this. I've counted at least five guides at the square so far. I'm the youngest I've seen, though, so tourists feel safer walking around with someone like me." He hits his chest, an act of bravado, and smiles. To a stranger he wouldn't look menacing. Felix is tall but wiry, with kinky blond hair and dark brown skin. His close-set eyes give him a look of cautiousness, hesitancy.

"You should show them the school," Marcos interrupts. "Show them the murals that we help to paint." The murals were part of an art project to get the students together. Groups of us were given designated walls around the outside of the school to paint over the graffiti. For weeks we met in the afternoons to paint. We were allowed to paint whatever we wanted, and Marcos chose to draw the three of us standing in front of one of the homes where we lived. Each of us looked down towards the other city that surrounded us. He drew the beaches, their white sand and crystalline waters. He drew the skyscraper buildings and countless bodies of people who in turn each looked up towards us, all smiling. It was beautiful.

"No one wants to see that, Marcos. They don't come here to see murals. They want to see filthy mothers on street corners feeding babies. They want to see shadows in alleyways of men holding guns. They're not going to pay to see a mural."

"We're all in it," Marcos continues. "It's nice now that it's finished. If I was a tourist I would like to see it."

"You're stupid," Felix counters. Marcos stops talking, his feelings clearly hurt. He looks to me to say something, to stand up for him, but I don't. When he realizes I won't he walks on ahead.

"Why'd you do that, Felix?"

"No one's going to pay to see that. You want me to lie? Then I'd have to take them and I'm trying to help us here. I know what they want and they want to see men with big guns. They want to hear stories like what happened at St. Cecelia's—"

"You told them about that? How could you do such a thing?"

"Why wouldn't I? It doesn't matter now that it's happened."

"It's wrong."

"Wrong? Someone else hurt those kids, not me."

"It's still not right, Felix, and you know it."

"Just let me worry about what's right, okay, brother?" He puts his arm around my shoulder but I shrug it off. He laughs and kicks my shin, hard enough for me to buckle down.

"Damn it, Felix," I cry out, bending over to rub my leg.

He keeps laughing and starts to run ahead of me, catching up to Marcos. "Hurry up!" he yells.

❉ ❉ ❉

For years there have been disappearances but only recently have people begun to notice. They have become more frequent, and before, where it was once adults, now it's children. We live in Morro dos Macacos, one of Rio's worst slums, or favelas, as they are known to us. Here war is raged between the police and gangs who fill the streets, taking over the grocery stores and shops, selling drugs openly in the streets, not afraid because for them there is nothing to be afraid of. In an effort to take back the city and control the escalating violence, the police shoot anyone, grown-ups and street children, anyone they believe to be a threat.

It started when three boys were found naked and beaten to death on the steps of nearby St. Cecelia's church. A garbage man was the one to call the police, finding them lying together in the shape of a cross. It was hours before the police arrived; by then someone had placed a blanket over them. When the police came, they used the blanket as a stretcher to carry each body away, dumping each one in the trunk of their car. They asked no questions. Even if they had, no one would have offered answers to what happened. Blood stained the steps for days. It wasn't until the next rain that it was washed clean.

Two weeks later a woman, the mother of one of the children, torched herself in protest. She was found howling through the streets in one of the city's richest areas. Her body began to shrivel as she ran, her face charring like coal. For the briefest of moments she ran until the flames overtook her and she stumbled to the ground—a heaping mass of burning flesh. Looming black smoke enveloped the streets as people covered their noses but not their eyes.

    The picture they took of her, the only one taken, was from one of the final moments before she fell. Her contorted body tilts forward, suspended in the air. Her arms are outstretched, grasping towards the space in front of her. She appears as if she's trying to escape the future she has set for herself, and in looking at the picture there's a moment when one begins to believe that maybe she had a different fate, that somehow she was able to escape the chasing flames at her back. In the favela people called her a spectacle. Neighbors mocked the image of her burning body. What woman would do such a thing to herself, they said, and for what purpose? It did not matter that her only child had been murdered and that the police had not only done nothing, but may have been the cause. She was a tale told of foolishness, gossiped about at the plaza where mothers gathered to wash their clothes. Didn't she know, they all scolded, and didn't she understand that this was life? What made her believe, they would say as they slapped their fabrics dry against the stone's edge, that her grief was any different?

* * *

    For kicks, Marcos, Felix, and I go to this store on Canal Street, towards the bottom of the favela where what shops there are exist. The owner is an old man who spends his time sitting on a stool behind the counter trying not to fall asleep. Pockmarks from acne scars hide behind his thick square-framed glasses. He wears collared shirts but each one is always stained, the rims of the collars faded and dirty.

    When I catch up to Felix and Marcos they are already inside looking around. This is what we do—one of us will buy something to occupy the owner while the others stay towards the back of the store. The store is small, crowded with packages and unpacked boxes of food that make it easy to block his view, even if he was to try to watch us. He never notices because it takes all his effort to ring up whoever's at the front. One of us will buy something, most often a bottle of coconut juice that we'll all share, and to pay we'll give the man change, tiny coins we'll pile up for him to count. We won't help and instead will watch as his feeble, tar-stained fingers pick up the coins. By the time he's finished the rest of us will have left, already haven taken the items we wanted. Once outside we'll share in drinking the coconut juice, letting the sweetness of it linger on our lips long after it's finished. It comes to us later as we wander through the roads of the favela, making our way to the tops where we live, that this is the only moment in our days when we are together and happy.

Today I am in the back with Marcos as Felix is at the front buying colas. He goes up to the counter. The man is sleeping so Felix stands there waiting. He looks at the assortment of candies and chocolates, picking up one after the other. He places some in one of his pockets and then after a moment takes it out. It is a game to him. He believes there is no threat, no looming consequences. I watch him as Marcos begins to place fruit in his bag, papayas and yams, and then he finds some packaged empanadas and stuffs those.

"I saw Marcela last night," Marcos says to me. "She was at the baile funk party near the west end."

"How'd you know it was her? Those places are skin to skin. It could have been anyone."

"It was her, man. I know it was her."

Marcela—with her golden breasts and thick, waist-long hair, is a queen in Felix's mind. She lives with her mother in the same section of the favela as us. Marcela will give it up to anyone, boy or man, as long as they've got money in their pockets to burn. Felix managed to score a date with her a few weeks back. A real one, at least that's what he tells us. Ever since, she is all he cares to talk about.

"Was she with anyone?"

"Of course, that's what I'm trying to tell you. She was grinding with Punto, had her arms wrapped around him so tight in that place you would have thought their bodies were built together. I haven't told Felix yet."

"Don't," I say. "We should go." At this I turn and see Felix walking up to us. He still has the change in his hand.

"That old man will be asleep until next year's carnival. Let's get what we want and get out of here." Felix starts picking up items, not even attempting to mask the theft. He smiles at us while he does it.

"We're leaving," I tell him, then nudge to Marcos to go. We start towards the door while Felix makes his way back to the register. He sneaks behind the counter where the brands of cigarettes are piled. He reaches for a pack but then the owner wakes and sees what Felix is doing. He takes hold of his arm and starts to yell.

"What are you doing? Are you stealing?" Felix tries to pull away but the owner has a good grip on him and won't let go. It becomes a tug of war between their bodies.

"Stop it, you need to let go!" Felix yells but the owner is not listening. Marcos and I stand there watching, too afraid to do anything, as Felix pulls and tugs on his arm.

Then, in one swift moment, Felix swings his arm and punches the owner in the side. He hits him again and in shock the owner lets go. Felix hits him two more times, once in the ribs and the other in the face so that his glasses crack and fall to the floor. The owner puts his arms up, making a cross against his face. "Stop," he begs in a low, cowering voice. I look at Felix. He has stepped back but is bouncing back and forth. His eyes are red.

"Let's go, Felix," I call out.

"No," he says. "I'm not leaving."

I go over to him and put my hand on his shoulder. Marcos stands by the door looking at us both. "Felix," I say softly, almost whispering his name. "We need to go."

"Fine," he says, his body now still. He reaches across the man and grabs the pack of cigarettes and puts them in his pocket. He nods at him before walking out.

Marcos does not walk with us. Felix and I walk along the paths together. I make sure to stay a few steps behind him, just in case halfway up the road he begins to change his mind.

※ ※ ※

This is not the first time I've had to stop Felix from the things he does. We're brothers, separated by only a year. Even though I'm younger, I'm the one who keeps us from getting into trouble. That's the way it's been since our father died two years ago. He died in his home, our home, when bullets came speeding through our walls. He was not the only one of us to get hurt, my brother got shot in his rib cage, but he was the only one who died.

"We need to teach him a lesson," Felix says to me that night. We sit by the small window that looks out from the favela. From our view we can only see the continuous stream of brick and mortar houses crowded onto each other like blocks. Black electric cables sprout from the ground and into every direction, like multitudes of spiders encroaching the city. "What if he had pulled me in? He would have called the police, or one of the justicieros, and they would have taken me."

"You scared him pretty bad. It wouldn't be right."

"What's right then? Look out that window and tell me what you know about right and wrong. This is what I know—I know that if you hurt me, I'm going to hurt you back much worse. I know that the sun rises each morning and sets each evening and the days go on with me stuck in this same place feeding the same hunger. Nothing gets easier."

"It's not all bad, Felix."

"Where are you living, man? Tell me because I'd like to go there. Where I'm sitting it's all shit. All of it. I want to be able to go outside and not see the trash pouring out onto the roads, or smell the stench of it when I get up in the morning."

"It would be nice to see the sky at least," I mumble back. "I would like to see the stars."

"You're crazy," Felix laughs and sits up in the dirt. With his fingers he draws on the ground, creating symbols and shapes. When he's finished he claps the reddened earth from his hands and looks at me.

"There," he points. "There is your sky and stars."

❄ ❄ ❄

If you were to ask me about my father's death, I would say that he died on a Friday night. He died in his home while sitting in his chair. He was not walking down the wrong alley or talking to men he shouldn't have. Bullets went through the cardboard walls and into his chest before he could even react enough to stand. A drug bust gone wrong was happening in the streets, which none of us knew then. We only heard the shots and instinctively got down, our cheeks pressed to the dirt, waiting and watching our father struggling to breathe until finally, stopping.

Then there is what comes after—how evenings now my

mother continues to wait by the door of our home. During the twilight hour she stands looking down the road, and I see the strain in her face when darkness comes and my father does not appear.

Some nights my brother shakes in his sleep, having spasms violent enough to jolt himself awake. I always wait for an explanation, for him to tell me about the dreams, but each time he only turns away and goes back to sleep.

I never wake him when he has those dreams. I stay up and listen to the thrashing of his body in the dark, the mumbled cries and low growls he makes that let me know he's not okay. I'm afraid that once he wakes I'll have to tell him what happened and again we'll both have to confront what we are trying to forget. We are boys—men. For us, there are rules to our sadness. So during those nights when I hear Felix across the room, I stay underneath my sheet waiting until he stops. He goes on throughout the hours, and when morning shines through and he opens his eyes and looks over at me I'll want to tell him, but I never say a word.

* * *

Maybe if those boys were the only ones, life would not have changed, but there are others—a group of seven kids were killed, found executed in an alley, a young girl was murdered and dragged to the river where they found her floating body. A friend from school was shot near his home while carrying a paper sack full of plantains. When they found him, someone had taken the plantains and eaten them, their peels scattered over his body like trash.

"It's the police," Felix had said. "They are trying to send a message."

The burning woman became a symbol, an image of rage against what was happening. Now they call her the great, burning star, after Revelations. She is something foreboding, a threat. People believe she is a sign of what is to come.

Stories are spun about her death to mirror the passage. People say that when she ran the fire lit up everything, the sight of her so strong, so bright that it was all anyone could see. An attempt had been made to put her out. Men chased her with buckets of water but she was faster than any of them. She flew through the city and when they finally found her, after she had collapsed by the riverbank, her body was still burning, an immense flame that did not spread but only burned in the spot where it rested.

Afterwards, when there is another death, when another child is kidnapped or someone disappears, it is blamed on her. "She was a sign," families cry, and she becomes their answer to explain away what is happening. She is the explanation for everything.

* * *

"I tell you, her body was like sugar," Felix says. He is talking about Marcela. "I think she's in love with me."

"What makes you believe that?"

"Can't I just know it? Can't I just feel it? She's in love with me." We are sitting together at a chicken bar. It is a small place with only a few chairs to sit outside. A small hut-like building is the restaurant. Next to it is a pen of chickens that trot in circles watching us. At a chicken bar you are able to pick out the chicken you eat. After the picking, the cook breaks its neck with one delicate, quick snap of his hands, and then takes its body to the hut where it is prepared and cooked. Felix watches as the cook snaps another chicken for a nearby customer. He drinks a beer.

"Listen, Felix," I stop myself.

"What is it?" Sweat beads form along his temples and slide down his face. He looks at me long and hard, waiting for me to say something.

"Marcos told me he saw Marcela with Punto."

Felix takes another drink and then puts his beer on the table. He licks his lips before responding. "When was this?"

I tell him everything that Marcos told me. In truth it is not much to begin with, but I tell him anyway.

"Why would you tell me this?" Felix asks. I turn away, biting the bottom corner of my lip. I had told him to make him angry because all I ever felt was anger toward him for never showing restraint.

"Because you are my brother," I tell him. "I thought I should."

I am not prepared for what comes next. Felix stands up, abruptly but calmly. He takes the few coins he has and pays for his beer. He looks around, surveying the land around him. He looks at me and without saying another word, starts to run, leaving me sitting there to decide if I should follow.

※ ※ ※

"What did you do with her?" Felix yells. When I catch up to Felix he has found Punto standing at the back of his club. He is wearing tight spandex shorts and a muscle shirt. A thick gold chain hangs from his neck. Felix has him backed against the wall. Punto puts his hands up, appearing defenseless, but his look is one of self-assuredness.

"Man, what do you think?" Punto says, spitting at Felix and wiping his mouth. "We played card games and drank punch. She took me to her room and showed me her dolls. Is that what you want to hear? Don't be surprised. You name someone and I bet she's been with him. Hell, you can name a her and I'd bet that too."

Felix stares him down, refusing to look away. He shifts his weight and kicks the side of his heel in the dirt.

"What, did you think that you were her one and only? That she was yours forever?" Punto smiles. "Did she tell you that? Did she rub her silky body close to yours, all the while her warm breath in your face, kissing you, and say that you were her only? I bet she did, and you believed her."

Punto laughs so hard that I can't look away from him. His arms are wrapped around his stomach, as if he's holding himself in. His laughter causes him to choke. Felix watches as Punto kneels to the ground with arms still clutching his stomach. Felix picks up a pile of rocks from the ground.

"Go ahead," Punto taunts. "Throw the rocks! You think Marcela will come back to you just by throwing stones? I know you're not that foolish."

Felix throws one at Punto's face but he blocks it. His laughter grows louder. Felix, not knowing what he should do, picks up more rocks and throws them, a continuous raining stream, at Punto but he blocks them all. He stays on the ground, his arms shielding his face.

Felix stops throwing and with this Punto starts to stand. "Is that it?" he says. "You give up so easily? Tell me because I want to know—was your father as foolish, as cowardly as you when he died?"

Before Felix can answer, Punto starts to run, but Felix is

faster and catches up to him before either of them have gotten down the path. Felix latches onto Punto's body and pulls him down. Together, the two of them wrestle in the dirt. Whatever Punto is, he is not a fighter, and he tries to pull Felix off but he's locked to him. I watch them roll around, dust clouding around like a tainted halo, until finally Felix lets go. Punto rolls on his back, wheezing heavily, while Felix stands. He kicks Punto's shoulders and his ribs. He kicks him in the shins and groin. Punto is trying to get up but he's out of breath and coughing. Felix keeps going, kicking and then bending over to punch him until Punto is curled like a child. Felix kicks his stomach and chest. He spits in his face and kicks his teeth until Punto's mouth spills blood. Even then it is not enough; he refuses to stop. He picks up the rocks and throws them, one by one, at Punto. This time he does not shield his face. Felix continues throwing long after Punto has stopped moving, until the only sound any of us hear is Felix's own labored breathing.

"What did you do?" I go up to Felix and grab onto his arms but he pushes me to the ground. I ask again, this time yelling it, but he ignores me. He wipes his hands on the back of his jeans. He kneels and places his hand on Punto's chest, waiting a moment to feel for a pulse before standing up.

"I can't tell if he's—" he stops himself. "Do you want to check?"

"Why'd you have to keep hitting him? You could have just left it alone."

"No," he says. "No I couldn't. I can't. You know I wouldn't have been able to." He looks down at Punto's bruised and bleeding body. "Help me," he says.

"To do what?"

"I don't know." He picks up Punto's body by the shoulders and starts to drag him. It takes a lot of effort to pull him and he doesn't make it far. He's heaving by the time he stops to drop his arms and rest.

"Help me carry him down to the river so no one will see. We can leave him there. If we hurry no one will see."

"Felix, I can't."

"Come on, I need your help." He picks up Punto's arms again and stands there, waiting for me, but I don't go over. I don't even make an effort to try.

"You shouldn't have done this, Felix."

"At least I've done something, unlike you. You don't do anything; you don't feel anything. I may be fighting the world but at least I'm part of it."

He stands there staring. Another step for either of us would mean acceptance, so neither of us moves. Each waits, refusing to make the choice for the other.

"I can't do this," I say.

"But you're my brother." He grips Punto's arms but doesn't go further. I wait, hoping for him to let go.

"Fine, leave before someone sees you," Felix finally says. "I'll take care of this."

❊ ❊ ❊

I make sure to walk the rest of the way home. I do not run, to run signifies trouble. To the police, someone who is running is either running away from someone who should be caught, or running towards something they should not have. I don't run but I keep a steady pace, stopping only when I catch a person on the street glance at me twice, and then I idle around, appearing aimless like a kid with too much time and nowhere to spend it.

A man comes up from behind me, wearing a cut-off shirt and jeans. "Hey," he calls. "Where are you going?"

I ignore him and start to walk faster. He follows me. I start to run but soon there are two men, three. They catch up and pull me down. When I stand back up they've surrounded me. One of them has a thick, keloid scar starting from his cheek going down his neck and into the covered parts of his chest.

"You were running and we want to know why," the second one says. "Were you causing trouble?"

"No," I say. "I need to go home."

"I think you were causing trouble," he says.

He has a gun and he pushes it into my back. He says for me to follow him; not knowing what to do, I let my body go limp and fall to the ground. The two men pick me up and one hits me in the gut. "You need to listen," he says. Then the other man takes handcuffs from his pocket and locks my hands behind my back. The cuffs are small and the cool metal scrapes against my wrists. He has a shirt that he rips in half, using part of it to tie over my face. It smells of sweat and dried blood.

"We're going to walk now," he says. The gun is pushed into

my back, nudging me to move. We walk long enough for me to lose my sense of direction, during which the men talk. We don't hurry down any one path, and the men act unafraid.

"We found your brother," he says. "Would you like to see him?"

"My brother," I repeat.

"Yes, yes," he slaps my back, causing me to stumble forward. He moves close to me and whispers in my ear. "We will take you to him. You want to see him, no?"

"Yes," I say.

"Good." At this we stop. I hear the sound of a car engine starting and the clunky pop of a trunk. Two men grab onto me, picking me up and hoisting me into the trunk. I'm too afraid to fight them. I let them put me in the car and close the trunk. I hear them laughing as they get into the car and start to drive.

There is no room in the space of the trunk. My body is curled up tight, knees to ribs, and I feel as if I am a snail inside its shell or wrapped inside a cocoon. It is a struggle to breathe in the hot air.

The trunk opens and the men pull me out. One of them takes off the blindfold and when I open my eyes I see that we have reached the bottom of the favela, near the coast of the sea. The wind blows its salty air against my skin. It is getting late, dusk approaches. As I look out towards the water I can see the richest areas of the city, the lights of twinkling hotels and buildings. I stare down at it and think of how beautiful it is from here, to be able to see it all.

"Where is my brother?" I ask.

"Soon," one of the men answers back, and he tells me to kneel. He stands in front holding the gun to my face and I am full of longing and regret. I am full of words unsaid, actions thought but never done. He says again for me to kneel but I continue standing.

"Look at you, fearless!" He laughs, showing the gaps of missing teeth from his mouth. "Unlike the others you aren't afraid. Unlike your brother."

He presses the gun to my skull. He wants me to close my eyes and cower but I stand upright, defiant. I keep my eyes open and stare straight ahead, looking into his own.

"Go ahead," I say. "Shoot."

DARREL ALEJANDRO HOLNES

Pagan

They bring the apocalypse,   these winged creatures,

     myrrh on parched tongues,   prayers

lambaste me dry,   rake scrapes skin,

     so much friction,   their language

         ignites a smokeless fire.

The air refuses   to hold what attempts to rise from flames:

     no red lights,   no sirens,   no saving runs.

We burn   without protest;

     a screaming smolder shows them you believe —

         this third world   special circle of hell,

and a god a black   hole

         hurling angels, trying to force peace

             with fired shots of *hallelujahs*.

But how else is power wielded   in a universe where

     nation is religion

         and *afire* is a sign   you are freed?

I want to be a heathen

     tasting blood beneath celestial bodies,

     polishing my teeth on their feathers,

       or in between this   and a gun-slinging seraph —

       a goddamned angel, some kind of half-winged being

brandishing knives;

one to pluck out stars,

       one placed at my bowels,   seppuku self surrender,

       a death the battlefield dignifies.

But I am not here to die   for your sins,   but to break

           the aching back of old believing, and screw this old maculate world,

        conceiving a newer one within her,

one where   its savior doesn't fall   at its genesis,   or die at world's end.

    A nest atop a city skyline —

Don't be scared of endings.

        Come, you too can be saved.

EDWARD ADAMS

Conspiracy

One bright day a monarch butterfly
in the fall migration to Mexico

paused in a Pennsylvania field
on the milkweed leaf where swayed his family.

He passed on lessons about flight
to his son, a creamy white egg.

He taught the usual things—to feel the sun's
angle as it moves across the wing,

to sense the pull of Earth's magnetic core,
to trust the subtle signals of antennae.

He whispered, too, this private mission:
My son, in Tennessee you will find

a wide lawn lush with zinnia, a pond,
and rocks to bask upon, an oasis

made for butterflies. There will be
two Adirondack chairs, a blue, a yellow.

In the blue there will be a man
his arm resting still, his sleeve pulled back.

In the yellow a beautiful woman smiles
glancing at her watch. You must land

on the back of the man's hand at seven
thirty-three because if you do

the man will win his wager and his wife,
so wonderful, will be especially sweet

to him when they retire for the evening
as you and your lady enjoy the butterfly garden.

Jane Vincent Taylor

On the Train, Traveling South, Looking North

I like to ride the car that travels backwards
so that junkyards and industrial parks become a metallic smear of color
                                        all smashed up like abstract painting.
I like to see the rumps of Jersey cows and baby calves with tiny ears
slip back into last summer's womb.

The guy behind me pulls the curtain closed.
He says it's nauseating, unnatural, to back up into where you're going.
He wants to move to a forward-looking seat.

Now Paul's Valley glides away, their mud, empty ballpark, the brickworks.
On the outskirts there's a spit of river
                 and I glimpse a man beside his battered car,
                              brushing his teeth, bending over, dressing.

This is no painting mounted on a gallery wall,
               more like a grainy movie of a past world
                            brittle, celluloid, silent, reappearing.
I'm not saying it's easy on the eye.
I sit here to see what I am leaving, what's lost to speed,
                            and where I almost was.

Martin Ott

Cloud Writing

As a grizzled man, I wrote with my fist
in steam, words sweating from the endless
practice, vapor forming around muscular
tongue, earned bullshit and dim desire,
the liquidity of a future still unspoken.
As a man, I penned a jet stream through
icy waters, unable to hold onto reason,
the cumulous career and babbling on,
the coughs of children and clunkers,
bones of a book blanketed in smoke.
As a young man, I became a dragon
in reverse, sucking fumes in motor
pools, spinning armored tracks over
mud flaps, smoldering with the desire
to hurt, scorched lungs and spirit quest.
As a teenager, I tried drawing desire
on the crooked parts of women eager
to make me feel like I was the soot
rising above the darkening snow banks,
the misshapen Michigan men to come.
As a boy, I sliced a line across the sky,
carving my stories in cloud blocks,
animal figures holding the shape of me,
the inky storm clouds brewing the way
to borders, to bombs, to future poems.

Fruits of Labors

My friend's new heart rests in a crevice
that housed the pacemaker; the wires fried
his old thumper like a zapped alternator,
doctors unsure this loaner will ever beat.
Blackberries float in a bowl on the counter,
separating out the spiders and veiny leaves.
Later, he tells me that he has gone to some
other place, a bifurcation of living and dead,
subterranean with a zenith, invisible susurrus
of some river, with trout, with kids splashing.
Thorns in those Michigan woods taught patience,
fingers careful not to burst the berry's juices.
There is one surgeon who goes in to save
his legs with a pinnate precision, arteries
flushed, and who stays at his bedside
after rounds, after the new heart reboots.
The taste of the jam boiled and jarred
from fly-filled afternoons fills us still.
He is unconscious for more than a week,
with dreams that make me wonder about
what will come after the jam disappears
from the pantry, when childhood is near.

LINDA PASTAN

Choosing Sides

In the war between the flowers
and the deer, my husband
has chosen sides, putting up a fence
at which two doe briefly stand,
looking in, locked out
in the wide world.

And though our woods
are newly filled with flowers,
safe now on their stems,
I think continually
of the deer who sleep
like penitents on their knees.

From the collection of the Managing Editor, photograph

Thomas Patterson

Room With a View, 1944

This is how you remember walking down the pavement
one Sunday evening late in September
8th Street to Coates' Pharmacy;
there is a bag you saw last night
that has ended up blown into a corner
from which there is no escape;
this is the *Altoona Mirror* declaring,
"Allies Roll Into France,"
opened on your grandfather's lap;
here is the summer unleafing to autumn
the blue aster on the porch the last to be doomed;
down the avenue is your mother's new home
the inside numb as a polished white corridor;
this is a town where your father once lived
the ballpark a mirage the players a dream;
these were the bells, Emanuelle
of Paroisse Notre Dame du Rhône
tolling the beginning of liberation;
this was your father's plane, *The Dreamer*,
coming back in flak-blacked two engines feathered
skidding across the wet tarmac;
these were the children on the bridge at Nîmes
playing at la marelle ronde
stumbling to the ground;
here is the hallway below the landing
where the iris are closing fall after fall
stiffening and darkening,
a prelude to forgiveness;
here is a room you walked back into
looking for something you must have lost;
here at this window you dreamed as a child
earth moon and stars
in perfect confluence.

Sally Allen McNall

Onset

The closer you are to combat, the less you are inclined to question it.
—Sebastian Junger

Unnoticed as the first order of what will later be seen
as a war, after rumor, in cafés, sightings on corners,
in the corners of our eyes, of the figures in camo and in
rags, in bomb-disposal suits, the Humvees, plain
finally as Katrina might have been plain, oh the names
we've used, named *here it comes now* now now scorched
brain, burnt skin, that supplicant shell sloughed off,
(shelled from a high corner) off a living body, a tell-
site of selves, tell me to shut up now or you will know
what I know, and I do, the damage is done and won't
be undone, the soldier home with a new unwanted face—
want won't get us far enough now as we plow
our personal dust or mud, the scrim of our half-ordinary life
halved for us as it tears stitch by stitch, is worn,
soiled, torn threads flapping like hearts wearing out
outside to in, like forests, if to be a forest is many,
fired, slow smoke to the many of the interior
poison enough to block the slow fire in sunlight
and we are not far enough from it, we breathe fire.

Wet with sun, plow, turn at row's end, plow,
like an ox turning at each stopped
field, in an airport, filling landing strips (while we wait)
with landfill, ourselves, others, distant distant others.

Benjamin Myers

Agincourt

My neighbor's son is jumping
from a helicopter into a field of poppies

that might explode. The father, proud
and worried, tells me about it one morning

as I water the wilting flowers
in front of our house and he stands

with a newspaper bag and a cup of coffee.
The elderly lady across the street comes out in her bathrobe

to smoke a cigarette and clip her roses, and I
ask myself if I could die to save her right to stand there

with her paper-white legs out-paling the morning
sun. In church they ask the soldiers to stand and the pews

become a time-lapse forest around me, redwoods
straight up on all sides while I sit low as a rotted fern.

I don't know what I believe about this war,
and I hear Branagh's King Henry declare that I

will hold my manhood cheap. My manhood is middle
aged and nearsighted and has read far too many books.

The National Guard convoys rattle the windows
of our little house when they roll down Main Street.

What can I say to those others, no different from me, really,
filing off into Afghanistan, like letters mailed to God?

AMY VANIOTIS

Fallen Marine

As if you will stumble
like a toddler. Like an old man
blindly. As if the ground will catch
your little trip, your tumble, your droll
mistake — as if I, as if I will be there
mouth wide laughing, clasping
your hand, bracing the whole
slight weight of my body,
heaving you back up.

Mark Weiss, photograph

LEE ROSSI

A Field

Yesterday, four-year-old daughter in hand,
I slalomed the farmers' market, crowds
of vegans, retirees, and trophy wives reaching parsley

and pomelos to vendors at their battered scales.
Espresso smell mingled with rotting vegetables.
We stopped for a trio of teenagers banging out cool jazz,

the two of us stones in a creek surging with spring flood.
And as we stood there, I felt myself receding, three decades,
to Nüremberg, the *Christkindlmarkt*, shoppers thronging stalls

of ornaments and cheap East-bloc toys (a giant goose-stepping
Nutcracker guarded the tree towering in the middle of the *Platz*).
Thirty years earlier the city, its half-timbered houses draped

with swastikas, had hosted the biggest shindig of the thousand-year *Reich*.
The woman I was with, I'd known her just a few weeks.
Like opposing armies, we'd been exhaustively mapping

each other's bodies. She had a limp—an early skirmish
with polio. Too weak to sustain a frontal assault,
she was in constant retreat, forcing me to attack

her flank or thrust from the rear. That was just between us.
To everybody else we looked smitten as new mittens,
holding hands, stuffing the other's cheeks with *Wiener Mandeln*.

Now we were out in the open, cool November on our lips.
We passed sugar beets heaped like cannonballs waiting
for the French attack. The field rose in corduroy welts

to a ridge where we could view the folded Hessian landscape
like Field Marshals on maneuvers. I tried to imagine the armies,
the millions of dead, but kept coming back to my own

unhappiness, other women I'd known,
my paltry triumphs of will, *der kleine Führer*.
I hadn't thought of that sleeping field for years,

or the woman, who slipped from my life as easily as one day
lapses into the next. But last night as I lay in bed with wife
and child, I saw it again, more real than their warm,

breathing bodies, saw it littered with autumn and our shadows
twining as we climbed. The sun at our backs caressed a last distant
hilltop, and then we stepped into darkness and numbing cold.

Mark Weiss, photograph

A Tour of Scotland: An Epithalamium

Gathered in a double-wide up a dry California arroyo,
four men survey a copse of golden bottles —
my bachelor party, number three.
My new brothers welcome me
according to the customs of their clan.
Tonight is special, nothing blended —
hurried glimpse from a Strato-liner —
we're crossing that narrow Northern land
on foot — one still moment, then the next,
starting in the heights, the air chill
and dense with mist, the liquor
molten caramel, sharp as flint,
Dalwhinnie to Glenmorangie,
a wee cup at each stop,
savoring the ascetic pleasures
of the moor, a breath of heather,
then something like milk wrung from granite.
Although it is invisible to our clouded sight,
we can smell the distant sea.
Slowly we work downhill,
Bladnoch and Glenkinchie,
a whiff of berry and oak,
the eternal, o'ermastering bite
of the sea. What we celebrate is
as fragrant, as difficult to hold
as the brute sea wind — a future
with their sister, my betrothed.
The squash of toe and heel
echoes in our bones, each thimble
a torch warming some unknown knot
of wariness and rage as we venture
in our wherry from island to isle,
Highland Park, Tobermory, and Talisker,
each smoky sip of peat, urine clear
and bright as brine. The daughter
of the house waits with sisters
and friends, tense with the mystery
of dishevelment, the body's ache
and rapture, what tomorrow brings.

Jamie Ross

Day Tripper

Because I'm an Eskimo. And free.
In the vestibule. Between two jolting cars
on the train to Winter Park. Here between
the snack bar and the Kandahar coach
next to the skis stacked like pick-up-sticks,
bamboo poles, flags, bibs, our boots,
and just below, the tracks. It's snowing.
The train rocks, jerks, shudders, clacks,
I can hardly hold on. Because I've got
one foot, and involvements, already
in the coach. Because I'm gripping
half an orange, two Cokes, two candied
apples, a Baby Ruth and a Snickers
as the cars careen the incline
to the Moffat Tunnel. I don't see much,
the soot and leaking water, my father
with his car keys giving me a hug, my
mother on the porch kissing me goodbye.
It's just a weekend ski-school; a slalom
course, a time-trial, to see if you advance.
If you advance, what do you get?
A ribbon for your parka, a new stripe
on your shoulder. The one Ellen Stark
likes to lean against, going home,
when she takes off her tasseled wool cap,
lets down her thick black hair. In the
eternally jolting car, the frayed red
velveteen seat, the veering cliffs and
snowfields, swaying roadcuts
and trees. All disappearing
into the six-mile dark.

REBECCA LEHMANN

Its Likeness Is the World

These are the hours where whisper meets word,
        where moment meets participant.
The whir of wind across the snow sends
        pulses of white through the air.
I think I see a dog outside the window—
        a trick of the light racing along
            the snowed-in riverbank.

That feeling though, of stepping outside a building into
        cold air, then stepping back into the warmth—
            as though our bodies are nothing
but melted snow and river mud.
I wait for you in lines like that, eating an orange,
        even though I don't like oranges.

I pull out the fruit's navel—it falls apart.
We could all come undone so easily.
The river outside the window
        freezes before my eyes.

Like this: all the light drained from the day,
        reminding me of every winter of my childhood.
The tin piepan my mother hid in a cupboard
        on St. Nicholas Day, filled
            with sunflower seeds, a Hershey bar,
        and an orange, which no one ate.
We weren't that kind of family.

I live with my winter hat on, try to read my palm
        by the waning light, but can't.
Go tell it to the Wastrel Moon, says the Snow-Filled Air.
That's how dusk turns into a blizzard.

Jim Daniels

Ducking

Outside, a man's shadow crosses the kitchen window.
Head lowered, he leans into snow angled against him.

Inside, I listen to an old funk song I danced to
back when. I mimic memories of a loose, drunken sway.

This morning, my son smacked my daughter with two snowballs.
The second, after she'd asked him to stop. I sent him inside

to pout while my daughter and I built a crooked snowman
who tipped over. Inside, he wrote me his first letter.

He hopes I have a bad Christmas. He will never write
or speak to me again until after lunch.

He is at the dentist now with his mother. My parents sent me
to my room to think about it, but I never did.

I danced to the mad music in my head that reeked of sin.
My son broke my heart for the first time today,

but I am a snowman for his love. I hope he has one
very tiny cavity. "The Genius of Love" is the song.

The announcer has a cold. The sky so low and heavy
with clouds, I duck. My daughter fell asleep

against my chest, and I laid her gently into bed.
I put my son's note on the refrigerator

hoping he will rip it down. I love snow.
He is seven. We live on Parkview

on the side of the street without the view
but I just saw a hawk land in the one tree

that rises above the apartments park side.
Branches like antlers of a giant reindeer

Jim Daniels

or the web of the world's clumsiest spider.
The hawk, a graceful ink blot against the white paper.

It killed a pigeon in our driveway last month.
The kids and I watched cartoons instead.

We spend our whole lives ducking, I'll tell my son
when he returns with no cavities and one apology.

Sometimes we call it dancing, I'll tell him.
Or maybe I'll just dance.

From the collection of the Editor, photograph

Jim Daniels

Charity's Anonymous Messages

tsunami, 2005

January rain. On the street, a man twists in on
himself, repeats himself slowly, each word

the heavy coin of asking. I'm not giving him
a quarter. What would a superstar do?

A giant wave erodes perspective.
If I could have a talk with Jesus today

I might ask him how to fix my garage door
or what's the precise location of the soul.

I've never hidden any money—just love letters
and drugs. The undertow of the heart yanks

us into fools or belly dancers or mimes
shouting a steady stream of obscene pieties.

A steady steam of breath rises against
January rain. It only hurts when I chew gum,

when I poke myself in the eye with a dull joke.
I haven't been hip in twenty years

and even then it was raining in January.
Give me snow to pack my soul

for the long journey. People ask how God
could make a wave like that.

My daughter's entering a little late here,
but she was born ten years ago today.

She's gotten her second digit.
The headlines scrape impossible numbers.

Jim Daniels

January rain. Mud in the street, rivers
flow like the low frequency of the voice

of Jesus or sea turtles or whales or three-
legged dogs. One man begs for himself.

He repeats himself slowly, each word
a giant wave.

Glenn Herbert Davis, photograph

Lisa D. Schmidt

Squirrel in the Attic

She chewed through wire mesh
to escape accusations
of wind and snow,

her empty belly bulging
like cheeks with uncracked nuts
plucked too early from my limbs.

She's ravaged her own fur
to build a nest in the darkness.

I imagine her retreat
between dusted trusses,
the rapid beat of her heart
cradled in a ship blown
off foreign shores.

And sometimes, when I'm asleep,
I hear stories she tells her pups
about a time when trees
were for growing green leaves
and the gardener answered prayers
with corn as yellow
as a young girl's hair.

Sky

Early evening in mid-February,
I looked up from the street of a city
still fresh with light
to see sparrows swooping together and unraveling
across sky that I became.

Now during tense afternoons
or dreamless nights,
part of me will remain
that shell-pink horizon
wild beings soared through.

My last hour on earth,
sky will breathe in me,
and wind-combed constellations of birds.
Let me remember the joy I felt
that moment in early spring
when I contained no boundaries.

Toward Winter

My neighbor speaks of them as "survivors," as one would
abused children sheltered in a safe house, or women
with large black bruises on legs, torsos, and arms.

But they are simply the plants I haven't yet killed
in the wasteland of my abandoned garden. Among
the straw yellow of unwatered grasses, bare stalks

where the deer have grazed, they alone
retain a vestigial green, a last flower.
I am ashamed to survey the rattling hydrangeas,

brittle lilies. Now I dig out what still lives
for a small window-box, set here along
a narrow, wind-protected ledge.

In this lessening season beneath its colder sun
late rising and slant, they are what's left.
We settle in, they and I, and hold on.

Barbara Swift Brauer

Missing Her

Somewhere out there tonight, he knows,
she is playing solitaire; her round face lit
in the glow of that eternal deck—as if Vegas Solitaire
could ever do her justice.

How he loved her bitten finger on the mouse,
the strap of her dress just off the shoulder
when she'd turn and tell him that luck was a carburetor
in need of sacrifice and steady maintenance.

Or tell him how the kings talked
in an Irish brogue, the knaves swaggered out
with a rodeo *savoir faire*. Now the red sevens are AWOL
and there's not an ace to be found.

He can't tell you what she brought
to this sad trailer or why she stepped into his life
on her way to someone else's. How she had a way
of making everything a part of the world *out there*.

Like a page of a monthly magazine,
a foreign newspaper, her accent always *á la mode*.
Oeufs for eggs, *le café*—he'd cook
for that woman again any time. Without her,

nothing here is ever different. No winners,
no losers. The computer, a blank blue.
The same sun rises every morning
and the wind hasn't shifted in years.

Jeff Gundy

Subjunctive on Burntside Lake

If you close your eyes and lie under the sky,
tiny creatures will begin to explore

under your clothes. And if you lie still
they will guide and direct you,

they will show you pageants and signs
in the clouds, sheep that safely graze,

concubines and cuckolds taking
blissful, nearly just revenge

in each other's arms. And your way
across the water will be clear,

and the boat that carries you
swift and quiet, and the oarsman

will steer easily over the deep water
and between the lovely islands, through

the channel to the far shore.
And when at last you offer the coin,

he will turn it back to you, and touch
your shoulder with his strong hand,

and ask only for your name.

Nostalgia

          To be absorbed again
into the essential green —
she wanted that, great wings
of spruce settling over the body,
the mind filled in
with shade.
          Nearby, an ornament
on its granite pedestal held in place
the ordered plots and shrubs,
the people stationed over the lawn
like carved pieces of a game,
all day the game
changing.
          There was a provided charm
as of some other country, the sun clicking
through heaven, the explosions
from a gun. And her grandfather, resting
as though he had fallen
asleep and it was someone else's blood, already
a memory, another story unfolding
the way pain is unwrapped
from a wound...
          her father saying
We heard cannon in the hills
shelling the city.
Crowds of soldiers
on the pier shoving
to get on board.
The ship, overloaded.
We pulled away.
The men panicked — some
were pushed off, others
shot themselves. I watched them
falling, watched
the waves, the bodies,
the darkening water.
Evening came to Sevastapol.

*It was 1920, Russia, seen
for the last time.*
      She considered
the light, the way it traveled
over the surface of the glass ball
which remained fixed
even as it appeared to be turning.
There was no beginning or end,
only loss circling back
again and again. Human longing reaches out
like that, she thought.
      In the sphere,
in her own reflection she could see
her mother, one hand held
to her eyes, looking
for the children, uncertain
they are safe. . .
      if that dream
would go on, if there were a green globe
with figures she could arrange, scenes
to be stopped, revised.

From the collection of the Editor, photograph

CLARK SMITH

The Bald Guy

At seventy, I can see myself as a small incident
in a world of big things,
a bald guy
beside the highway pissing into
the tailwinds of sadness and love,
kindness and desire
that still pass by—
a senior perhaps in need of help
if not right now, then
not much past Nebraska.
   There's a baffling and
zany contraption
seventy can place in the way—
pot-bellied traffic barrels,
flashing yellow arrows the size of minivans
forcing me into a lane I didn't choose.
Just yesterday, stopped,
leaning out the driver's side window
like a cocker spaniel
I pled with the flagman
for a second chance,
knowing there's no such thing
but doggedly thinking too
that all that oatmeal, flax, Flomax, Lipitor, salmon and walking
is just like the Bible—
it has to mean something.
   Ever since my freckles disappeared
beneath a blizzard of liver spots
I have been wondering
where I sign up for an easier life
though I never expected one to emerge
from the bedragglement of my upbringing,
which sent me running for cover, a good move,
not the bullet train through sex, romance, money,
cars and countrysides I imagined into
the endless cloverleaf of my fifties,
bumpy at times, two bad accidents,
but still fun

though always the rearview mirror
clouded by what came before,
objects that appeared to be further off
than they really were
as if there were no choice
except to settle for a reflected long shot,
me, as always
only a tenth or less
the height of the whole picture,
back in my car and driving again
but like all of us, inconsequential,
the past closing in from behind
like a force five tornado
sucking up a Kansas farm
and whatever it was I thought of myself
that season I was young.

Glenn Herbert Davis, photograph

Dian Duchin Reed

Out of Sight

In back of the head
is where bald spots hide
and labels unfurl from the necks of shirts

making us wonder from time to time
what's hidden on the far side of our own moon,
that is to say, what it would be like

to see ourselves as others see us

which is what Robert Burns wrote
after watching a louse crawl across
the back of a seated lady's elegant head

though this kind of farsight would have to
include the unconscious back of the brain
where we'd like to think we can jettison

the unthinkable and dump it out of mind,
despite the fact that it often orbits
in clear view behind us.

Kathleen Kirk

Before I Can See

There is a time now, in the morning,
before I can see, when words squinch
and blur, beside themselves

with doubtful import. You'd think
I'd learn not to try to read or write
at that hour, but it's what I do.

I can't stop now. Superstitious worry
will not spare me any kind of blindness.
I know that. But still I trust my own

handwriting, at its hover and slant
just above the diary line, and I believe
the opening of possibility in the words

trembling without fear on every page.

A window shalt thou make

to be a thing commanded to be made
    cut out of a thing commanded to be made
to be cut from yellow wood,
sealed in pitch
to be the only way out for so long,
    the only open way
to be above the door, as commanded,
    the closed door
to be the way to death
    or a way to eventual life
to be a detail in the architecture
    of a myth
to be what they looked through,
    what they yearned through
to be the opening to the senses,
    what seen, what heard, what smelled, tasted, touched
to be what the wind came through,
    what the rain came through, the sun
to be what the raven went out through,
    and the dove, and the dove again, the dove
to be what the dove came back to
    with an olive leaf
to be this locus of the myth,
    the frame for the dove

Molly Tenenbaum

During the Night, Mom Has Unpacked a New Box

I never see mom in this house
where she lives and I live,

but air moving through open windows
lifts the cardboard motes of boxes,

ruffles the tissue of wrappings.
Where she lives and I live,

where I never see her,
a carton with open flaps

has been left by the sink,
and in the drainer, flutes

of white glass, opaque,
what they call milk glass, with gold paint

blurring the rims like lipstick
on old-lady lips, glasses I know I saw,

believe I saw, from below on a high shelf
when I was small.

But they don't make this kind of glass
for champagne—it's for a hobnail tureen,

candy dish, cake plate, it comes in pairs
for cruets, cream and sugar sets.

Not in these thick champagne trumpets
here in the morning, so near

my dream of water never reaching the spout, that pours
from a rift in the seam of a pinched clay kettle

I made myself, that won't fill
past the hole.

And while I slept, crumple by soft
paper crumple, she was unwrapping her vessels,

Mom, in this house, where I never see her —
paper-dust like sleep hair on my head,

milk-shadows moving, gold of my parents
laughing together before I was born.

Daniel K. Tennant, *Here Today, Gone Tomorrow*,
Gouache on Museum Board, 28" x 34"

LAURELYN WHITT

Holding On

Here is an elegy for the vestigial

   wings of emu and kiwi
     stirring when the flightless
     remember flight.

In the semilunar fold of the human
   eye, a third eyelid
    withers.

Something in a minor key to soothe
the remnant, a lament

   aligned like an element
    in magnetic flux once
     a field has passed

   or magnetite in the beak of a
    migrating bird tugged
     by the world below.

Music to console the residual, in
   tempo *sostenuto*. Composed
   in pulses. Beating hearts.

A song for what remains.

Geri Rosenzweig

From Night's Libretto

for Mel

Since they washed your mouth
with the morphine
of forgetfulness

I've taken to lying down
with the morning
star's shadow,

haven't stitched the rent
in my coat, nor
brushed the dust from my shoes,

dust that bears me
from one end of the hour
to the next,

dusky vowels
we'd lift from night's libretto
no longer blossom

among the little bones
of my ears;
you should be here,

your skin fragrant
with the almond soap I bought
yesterday.

I Want to Wake up Again

Bring me the red sundress
    my mother ran up

on her sewing machine
    one summer night

while Radio Luxemburg
    delivered exotic

bouquets of music
    to her small kitchen,

bring me the red sundress,
    I'll kick off

my dusty sandals,
    step into one

of the white sailboats
    she hand-

stitched to its hem
    while I slept

on the shore of childhood;
    I want to wake up again.

INES P. RIVERA PROSDOCIMI

Love Letter to an Afterlife

Start as a slow rocking into sunset, and be my Mama's playing.
Each piano key: a rising and falling like a lung.
Be music when it came easy and be Sundays.
Sundays for milongas, and the day we speak with our dead.

When night comes like a woman letting down her hair,
be a confirmation: a royal flag calling the carnival—
where a throng of guloyas dance infinitely,
horns and tusks tearing open a childlike fervor
I'm chasing now.

Be Bonao's green. The low hush of the reeds,
the river nearby, the water slapping the rocks.
Be the indigo sky above the women
lunging backwards, throwing coins
and prayers, into the river snaking below.

Then be a cigua, that tiny simple bird, and lead me
to a field of poppies. Be the red splash
across those blossoms. Be the wind—like the flick
of a horse's tail—as I walk among those flowers
and there is nothing, nothing but them.

Vince Sgambati

Grave Companions

On damp rainy days when umbrellas and hurried steps spoke of solitary lives, Sal found solace in the diner beneath the Oxford Avenue El. From a booth and sitting on a cracked vinyl bench with his forearms pressed against a chipped Formica-topped table where most of the yellow had faded into white, he contemplated patrons shaking loneliness from their coats and hats and sometimes from their hair, making luminous haloes like in the pictures of saints on his bedroom dresser, where his wife once lit tall slender vigil candles with matches pressed between her not so slender fingers. Customers wearing glasses removed them and wiped beads of water from their lenses and others simply dabbed their eyes so as to see without rain, because rain isolated them. Sometimes Sal perched on a stool at the counter and remembered holiday meals when his extended family and friends crowded around the dining room table made longer with four leaves, and his wife was the pulse of the feast, not just because Tillie was in constant motion replenishing empty plates, but because with great animation she also fed the family stories and laughter. And when sitting at the counter among strangers reading newspapers and drinking coffee, Sal hungered for those stories and for that laughter and for Tillie.

He looked beyond his quivering mug of hot coffee and spotted a woman sitting at a table for two in the front window where the name Scarpentonio's was stenciled in reverse, and he wondered if it was the steam from his coffee or tears that moistened his eyes, for it's one thing to sit alone in a booth or at a counter, but quite another to sit alone at a table for two where the sole chair facing you is pointless. She smiled at him, not Tillie's smile that once made him real, but a warm smile nonetheless. Years ago, Sal would have blushed, but at his age a young woman's smile means just a smile so he managed a thin curve of his lips in response, then looked down at his plate of eggs and home fries.

The diner smelled of damp raincoats and drenched umbrellas and of coffee and bacon and of hot grease from the grill and of the hot layers of paint that bubbled and peeled away from old radiators like crumbling memories, and he pushed the eggs from one side of his plate to the other, then turned down his hearing aid because the noise of china and silverware overwhelmed conversations and he wasn't really interested anyway. His cup rattled and though he couldn't hear the train he knew that it had just left the Oxford Avenue Station, and he noticed that the young woman with the warm smile was no longer sitting at her table for two and he imagined her riding the departed train as it rattled past shaded windows in apartments above shabby storefronts and then descended underground where it's too risky to give away smiles.

Sal didn't ride the subway anymore or buses or even drive his car but a few blocks. He drank the last bit of coffee, and then stared into the empty mug as if searching for answers in its spidery veins.

"More coffee, Pops?"

He turned up his hearing aid but lowered his eyes away from the lettering *Under Construction* stretched across the waitress's belly and his brow creased and his lips disappeared in a frown, "No thank you, I have to say goodbye." The waitress dropped the check next to his left hand where a gold band girdled his gnarly ring finger, and she moved on without taking the time to understand.

Under the cavernous el of iron and wood and cement where rainwater dripped as if from a thousand stalactites, Sal opened his black umbrella and shuffled across the avenue and beyond the el, where rain turned to drizzle and where he was cautious not to slip in the puddles of oily rain mixed with florets from Norway maples or to trip over ridges where the sidewalk had yielded to tree roots and winter ice. He passed brick and stucco and vinyl-sided houses, one-family or two-family, with wrought iron fences and scrolled grates on basement and first-floor windows and "beware of dog" signs even if no dogs lived there. Some windows were decorated with cardboard cutouts of Easter bunnies and colorful eggs and crosses with white lilies, while in small front gardens, fenced with brick and wrought iron, daffodils and tulips bobbed before concrete statues. A few umbrellas rushed passed him, most likely on their way to the train station. Across the street an umbrella moved as slowly as Sal's and beneath it was an old woman dressed in black, pulling a cart filled with yesterday's headlines.

A private ambulance was parked in front of Rocco's house, and Sal, though mostly pleased that he made it in time, felt distraught by its sight and its implication; he didn't notice Angie sitting in her son's car. Before Rocco's stroke Sal had visited them often and usually overstayed his welcome, but they felt sorry for Sal and Angie always cooked more than enough supper anyway, and, after Sal no longer drove except for a few blocks, Rocco would drive him to Saint John's Cemetery to visit Tillie's grave. Sometimes Angie joined them and on their way home they'd stop for coffee at Dunkin' Donuts; occasionally she packed a lunch, and after the cemetery they parked at a favorite spot where they watched boats out on the bay and planes leave and arrive at LaGuardia Airport and trains pass in the distance, and they spoke about what was past and finished each other's sentences. After Rocco's stroke, Sal visited them only once and he told himself that trying to hold a conversation with Rocco frustrated his old friend, but he called Angie every Sunday to see how things were.

Angie lowered her window and called out to Sal through the drizzle. He was unable to discern the sound of raindrops tapping on his umbrella and cars splashing by from the sound of his name, but he spotted Angie waving.

"They're inside putting Rocco on a stretcher." Angie brought a tissue to her aquiline nose. "My son paid for a private ambulance. He thought his father would be more comfortable." She ran her thumb along the back of her wedding band. "I don't know."

Sal leaned closer to the car and held the umbrella over the open window to shield Angie. "Young people have their own ideas. This is good, Angie. You have a good son."

As if unsure, she nodded her head but shrugged her shoulders. "It's too much for my son to keep driving down here. He's got his own family to worry about. I'm not so good about paying bills and getting things fixed. Rocco took care of all that." Again she shrugged, but also extended her hands, palms up like the concrete statues Sal had passed along the way and as if to say it was beyond her control. "I guess we'll sell the house, but I feel bad for the tenants. They've been good to us."

"One thing at a time, Angie." Sal wished he had offered to help Angie with bills and day-to-day maintenance, though he knew that Rocco would have disapproved. Friends, no matter how close, aren't family.

Angie pointed to the front of the two-family brick house where sixty-three years ago she had moved in as a bride. Arched over a stretcher, a huge man backed out of the front door and lumbered down the steps of the brick stoop. Rocco's right arm was extended up over his eyes, and a second smaller man supported the end of the stretcher beneath Rocco's head. Behind them, Rocco's son locked the deadbolts of the inside and wrought iron storm doors, then followed the procession to where the attendants set his father's stretcher onto a gurney. The son opened an umbrella over his father, and Sal remembered a much younger Rocco with arms that could lift a case of olive oil and swing it onto one of his broad shoulders as if it were a down-filled pillow. When they were boys, long before Sal took over his father's bakery and Rocco his father's grocery, Sal both admired and envied his friend's strength and—back then—Rocco's prowess at baseball. Across the street from where the ambulance waited there was once an open field and Sal and Rocco and a band of first-generation American boys played baseball in the trampled-down weeds on humid summer evenings until the moon and fireflies were the only light and hungry mosquitoes feasted on the boys' bare legs. Sal recalled the crack of the bat against the ball and the smell of low tide wafting in from Howard Beach, as he watched his old friend jiggle across the broken sidewalk. He left Angie to her tears and approached the back of the ambulance where the two attendants were about to lift the stretcher from its gurney. Rocco's son motioned for them to wait.

"Hello, Mr. Beltrani," he said, and they shook hands as their umbrellas met over Rocco, and Rocco lowered his arm away from his face and clasped the hem of his friend's jacket. The stroke had taken Rocco's language and left him with only a few nonsense words like *nippy* and *fenzo*. The attendants were wet and impatient. "I'm sorry, but we have to go, Mr. Beltrani," Rocco's son apologized. "We have a long drive ahead of us."

"Of course. I understand," Sal said, and leaned closer to his friend. "Don't make your son crazy." And he thought to kiss Rocco's forehead, but remembered doing the same to Tillie before the undertaker closed her casket and it felt too foreboding. Instead, he squeezed his friend's free hand.

Rocco released Sal's jacket and slowly waved the tips of his fingers, and as the attendants lifted the stretcher into the ambulance, he glanced back and, the way old couples mirror each other, he made the same shoulder and hand motions that Angie had made only a few moments earlier, and then he stretched his arm back over his eyes and his sleeve absorbed his tears.

"Can I drive you home, Mr. Beltrani?" Rocco's son asked as he pulled a handkerchief from his pocket.

"No, thank you," Sal answered. "My car is parked on the avenue. I walked here from Scarpentonio's."

Through curtains of drizzle, Sal was unable to see if Angie waved, but he waved back nonetheless as the ambulance pulled away from the curb and the car followed, and in the finality of the moment he thought of Tillie and was reminded that since Rocco's stroke, he hadn't visited her grave, and the two months felt like forever to someone who in the thirteen years since his wife's death and until he stopped driving his car but a few blocks had visited his wife's grave every day. There was his hospital stay for prostate surgery and the occasional holidays that were spent with his daughters, but such times were the exceptions. Tillie had died when Sal still owned and operated his bakery, and every day at lunchtime, he bought a sandwich and cream soda at Rocco's store, then drove to the cemetery. Next to Tillie's gravestone, he unfolded a small red campseat that he kept in the back of his truck, and he ate his lunch and if no one was around he talked to Tillie. Over the years he befriended a few regulars—mostly old-timers and Italians—who visited the cemetery on weekends or for holidays and special occasions. They'd nod to each other, exchange a few words, and then go about their business of caring for their loved ones' graves and whispering prayers; and the truck with *Beltrani's Bakery* stenciled across its side panels became as much a fixture at Saint John's Cemetery as the gravestones and mausoleums and, on cold or rainy or snowy days, it provided shelter for Sal to sit in while he ate his sandwich and drank his soda and talked to Tillie. More than a few of the regulars felt a tinge of grief when Sal replaced his truck with a Buick (after he sold his bakery)—just another reminder of loss, like a mound of freshly disturbed soil or a name added to a gravestone.

With Rocco and Angie went Sal's hope of visiting Tillie's grave, which felt the same as no longer being able to visit Tillie. This feeling had plagued Sal ever since Rocco's stroke, but as he waved beneath the solitude of his umbrella, the loss was suddenly unbearable, reminiscent of the feelings he had suffered almost thirteen years earlier when he stopped home for lunch to surprise Tillie with fresh warm Easter bread and a pot of hyacinths. His hands were full, so he pushed open the kitchen door with his hip, careful not to crack the pastel-colored hardboiled eggs peeking out from the warm golden braid of bread or to crush the grape-smelling flowers. Tillie would place the flowers at the center of the kitchen table, then make espresso coffee while Sal sliced the bread and the aroma in the kitchen would be strong and sweet. They'd sit at the table and sip the espresso from demitasse cups that they had bought years ago in a little shop on Mulberry Street and spread whipped butter on chunks of warm bread and Tillie would begin, "This reminds me of the time we…" Something about the moment would spur one of Tillie's stories and Sal would smile and nod and he'd add a detail or two, and their reminiscing would become a dance of words and nods and laughter, and their rapport would spark more intimate feelings and they'd move from the kitchen to the bedroom. But instead, when Sal entered the house, there was no sound of humming, or of Tillie's stockings rubbing against her skirts as she rushed about the rooms, and when he called out her name there was no answer. Unwashed breakfast dishes sat next to the sink and Tillie in a cream-colored slip trimmed with lace and her hose balled up in her right hand lay across her unmade bed. Sal stood at the bedroom door holding out the Easter bread and hyacinths as if expecting his wife to rise and take her gifts from out of his hands.

You didn't say goodbye, Tillie, Sal thought as he watched what in the distance appeared to be a phantom ambulance turn the corner onto the avenue under the Oxford Avenue El. No siren, no need, Tillie was gone. But then he remembered that it was Rocco's not Tillie's ambulance. Her silent ambulance had left thirteen years ago, a long time for Sal to wake up each morning regretting that he was still here.

❊ ❊ ❊

Red lights provided respite and he took deep breaths and gave himself pep talks and when the light turned green, slowly he raised his right foot from the brake and eased on the gas, anticipating the relief of another red light. Street names, stop signs, traffic, pedestrians, and kids on bicycles competed for Sal's attention. Like when he turned off the coffeemaker on the kitchen counter or took his medications, he spoke his actions aloud as if reminding a child to complete his chores: "turn left on Woodhaven… watch out for that little boy . . . don't get too close to the bus." Three days had passed since he said goodbye to Rocco and Angie, and since then all he had thought of was that he had to tell Tillie he could no longer visit her. Its being the anniversary of her death gave him added motivation to make a final visit. He had thought of calling one of his daughters—they both lived in Manhattan—to drive him to the cemetery this one last time, but he quickly dismissed the idea. They were slighter versions of their mother in appearance and in other ways, as if calorie counting depleted them not only physically but also emotionally. They lacked their mother's generosity. The way Tillie was always the first to show up and the last to leave and offered food and laughter and tears and stories as if she were a human cornucopia, her daughters mostly offered apologies. Sorry, but I have a meeting, or my husband is working late, or the kids are busy, or I forgot but we already made plans. Sal loved and was proud of his daughters, and he tried not to blame them for not being their mother, but he knew not to depend upon them.

He drove beyond his imagined limits for the first time in almost two years, crawling in the far right lane of an eight-lane boulevard—four lanes traveling east and four lanes west. As a boy, Sal had biked the eastern route to the beaches when this concrete boulevard was a gravel road that meandered through acres of marsh where ibis and osprey and heron and egret enjoyed the vast wetlands. He had seen the first two-lanes paved and every subsequent expansion since, just as he had seen wooden sidewalks become concrete and gas streetlights become electric and open land become rows of houses and stores and schools and churches and synagogues on a grid of streets intersecting avenues. And this grid had been imprinted on his brain and revised multiple times and each time his brain rewired and accommodated, but as he drove west on Woodhaven Boulevard to Saint John's Cemetery the once familiar street names and landmarks seemed strange. Like the gravel roads he had biked as a boy, his thoughts meandered through the marshes of his memories. "Are you sure?" he asked himself aloud. "This doesn't seem quite right."

In all, Saint John's was about five miles from his house and he had already driven halfway there when a Camaro peeled out around Sal's Buick. Startled, Sal glanced to his left, but within the blur of red and chrome he could barely make out the young driver and the driver's extended middle finger, before the Camaro swerved in front of him, and Sal, as if summoning some forgotten reserve of energy, jerked his steering wheel to the right and slammed on the brakes, just missing a parked taxicab. He thought that it was the vibration of the steering wheel that made him shake so violently as he rolled up next to the curb in front of the taxi and parked, but after letting go of the wheel he continued to shake. His head sank back into the headrest and his eyes closed. Again, he was startled, but this time by someone rapping on his car window. It was the cabbie whose car he had almost sideswiped and Sal attempted to lower his window, forgetting that he had turned off the ignition.

"Open your door," the cabdriver yelled and Sal obeyed.

"Are you okay?"

"Yes, I think so," Sal answered, but his body continued to tremble and he was beginning to sweat.

"I saw that son of a bitch cut you off. Thought you were gonna slam right into me, but you didn't... no thanks to the jerk in the Camaro. You got pretty good reflexes for an old guy.... Are you sure you're okay? You don't look so good. Maybe I should call an ambulance."

Sal noticed the cabdriver pull a cell phone from out of his jacket. "No, no, I'll be okay. Just let me step out of the car and get some air." The last thing he wanted was to wind up in an emergency room. If he was going to die, let it happen near Tillie rather than in a hospital. Something about the cabdriver's strong grip as he helped Sal out of his car made Sal feel frail and incompetent and reminded him of visiting Rocco after the stroke and how Rocco had cried, and Sal feared that he might do the same in front of this stranger.

He leaned against his car, small in the shadow of the Samaritan cabdriver, who was as huge as the attendant who had helped carry Rocco's stretcher to the ambulance.

"I'm feeling better already, and I'm glad that it stopped raining." But from the cabbie's expression—an expression that crossed the faces of most people Sal spoke to lately—he knew that he had said something wrong, and after he glanced at the dry pavement realized his mistake. "Guess I'm still a little shaky, but I'll be okay ... really."

Evaluating the situation, the cabdriver stared at Sal, then looked pensively to the right, then back at Sal again. "Think you can stay here alone for a minute, I'm gonna run in that store and get you something to drink."

"Yes, but there's no need for . . ." Before Sal could finish protesting the cabdriver disappeared into a small deli, the front window papered with faded handmade signs advertising sandwich specials, bagels and knish. Sal turned but could barely read the words in the narrow storefront window except for "knish." And he remembered a time or he imagined a composite of many times when he and Tillie ate at Nathan's in Coney Island after hours of amusement park rides and games and he would carry a tray piled high with hotdogs and french-fries and a knish for Tillie—sometimes with his daughters hanging on either side of him—back to where Tillie sat against a backdrop of lime-green walls punctured with a row of porthole windows. She looked beautiful to Sal, like the feasts she prepared—colorful and bounteous. Her shiny hair was blacker than her large eyes and her full lips were redder than the blush of her cheeks and her polka-dot sundress barely contained her ample breasts.

Still leaning against his car and staring at the rush of traffic, he realized that it wasn't only Tillie that he missed, but he missed being the one to carry the tray. He missed who he was with Tillie and who they were when the girls were young, and he also missed yeast and eggs and flour and never skimping on ingredients or on the time that it took to bake perfect breads for loyal customers. And he missed a way of living that had to do with priorities and being thorough and being there when you should be there and knowing that for family and friends you should always be there, and it had to do with visiting his wife's grave, even though his daughters told him that Mama's not really there, which was just another excuse for not doing what you should. Then he thought of Rocco and of visiting him only once after his stroke, and Sal felt ashamed and wondered if his daughters took after him more than they did after their mother.

And he also wondered if hyacinths were in bloom beneath the name Filomena (Tillie) Beltrani carved in pink granite. Last fall, Rocco had handed him each hyacinth bulb one at a time while Sal knelt on one knee and carefully planted the bulbs in the soil before Tillie's gravestone, as carefully as folding eggs into flour. With one gnarled hand pressed against the cool granite and with Rocco's support he was able to slowly get back on his feet again. He regretted that Rocco and Angie would never see the hyacinths in bloom or smell their grape fragrance and most likely neither would he, and he felt old and foolish for having tried to drive to the cemetery. Then it dawned on him that the cabdriver could drive him the rest of the way to Tillie's grave. In fact, this could become routine—maybe not every day, but once a week. Why hadn't he thought of this before? Cabdrivers drive old folks to church and to supermarkets all the time. Why not to cemeteries? When you outlive your peers, you have little choice but to depend on strangers. And he imagined the cabdriver and him stopping at Dunkin' Donuts and even at the place where he and Angie and Rocco used to park by the bay. Then he recalled the cabdriver helping him out of the car and the expression on the cabdriver's face when he misspoke about the rain and he hated what he had become and he wanted the cabdriver to know that he wasn't always like this. *Just ask Tillie*, he thought. And then he thought again of the hyacinths and he thought so hard that he saw their dense clusters of bells and smelled their grape perfume and he was glad that they were in bloom.

RACHEL INEZ LANE

Dyslexia is a Lonely Cloud

Whenever I have to read out loud, when my thoughts
      blend together, and words stumble
from my mouth like a drunk in torn jeans, weeping
      for the right words to say—I get all red,
then everyone asks if I'm allergic to something,
      and I say—*Coffee,*

I'm allergic to coffee! "How awful," they say,
      and I go, *I know, how awful.* But please, let me
explain how my mind will always be an orphanage
      for deformed letters, pieces born
without a puzzle, how "felt" is forever "left"
      and "left" is well, a little bit
          cosmic, a little bit—

like Scrabble. When I was little, I'd hide the I's
      and Y's inside my dad's guitar,
place S's on my eyelids, stretch out on the carpet,
      and sing lyrics the wrong way—
          but there's more

to the vowels I can't see or maps I can't read.
      There are times when my heart beats
upside-down, and its valves form inlets that bleed
      out to my stomach. When you wrote
saying you were trying not to leave, I read you
      were dying not to leave. So when
          you left, I was so—

thrown, like when I got lost trying to find your house
      at night—you got mad, and I
got nervous, because all I thought I did was try

      to memorize your storyline. And then
you ask me if I'm allergic to something. And I say, *Nuts,*
      I'm allergic to nuts. "How awful," you say,
and I go, *I know, how awful,* but maybe I'm
      just being sensitive, or maybe I'm

a bully with a spitball who's taking aim at some poor
      fat kid, who simply wants to split
a bag of Doritos, who I won't see again, because
      at sixteen I dropped

out of high school—managing to spell my own name
      wrong on the dismissal form in
ink. The secretary rolled her eyes, then asked, "Are you
      allergic to something?" And I said, *Chocolate,*
I'm allergic to chocolate." How awful!" she said,
      and I said, *I know*. It's awful,

my GRE scores are lower than my credit score,
      combined. I lack coordination, have issues
with zippers, so I'm left flailing about your room pretending
      to take notice of your wall art when all I want to do
      is take my clothes off—and this
      is how I'll die—

in a flaming car wreck, my hair on fire, chunks of brain,
      now Jell-O, glistening against the dashboard
as my body death-rattles to the frozen requiem of my GPS
      reminding me that it's—*Recalculating. . .*
      Recalculating—and you'll feel rotten

for yelling so much, but I called it passion every
      time you did, because all I wanted to do was hold you
until you were a screen print on my T-shirt because,
      Jesus Christ, you were so clever—you
      could spell "spaghetti,"

but everything is okay now, because after you left, I was
      at the library reading Wordsworth in the corner,
and when I got tired, I looked down, and the words began
      to move, sail along the page, break into lakes,
      and I started to read—

      I wandered lonely as a cloud
      That floats on high o'er valves and hills
      Continuous as the stars that shine,

and it was lovely. All those words touching, bodiless
        spirits, getting lost, just to find a new way home,
recalculating, and for the first time I understood
        something better than anyone, better than you,
            better than language itself.

From the collection of the Editor, photograph

Becky Kennedy

Returning

It was early autumn
yes, the trees warmed along
the house and the sun
guttered through them

though the clouds said rain
and the spreading birds
and the leaves blown
into the street

and the hard cold knock
of acorns and the looseness
of fruit and the endless
tumbling of leaves

and the emptied branches
and the paths of them
rising arrested
yes, you

gone and the sky
behind like a blue door
unlatched
flung wide

T. Alan Broughton

Doorways

They are not what I see since always I'm looking
past them to the next room. Sunlight drapes chairs,
a table, but the window in that room also offers
passage to maples, a bank of green. Where I sit
the room surrounds me, but I am already elsewhere
despite the floor, a hard wood bench under thighs.

All my life doorways have let me by, hinges
giving way to the twist of a hand. I pass through
the frame into next moments not even gathered
wholly in that space because in the wall there is
another opening, perhaps the illusion of walking
through to a porch, a landscape of lawn and field
falling away to dusky pond that mirrors evening.

See how the sun is sliding downwards, the sky
is a doorway to the room of stars, the stars
are too dim to reveal the widening portal
expanding like a lens, an ever-opening eye,
and that too is only a glimpse of room after room
that might be nothing more than where I am now,
believing I am myself when I too am not
what contains me but only the next threshold.

Tree House

Green was in woods, and wind stirred them
so light could always make new landscapes,
and mornings of waking to a name called
by familiar voices was slow, the name slow
in becoming one's own and new each morning—
or so it could seem, as if the father and mother
who called conspired to make it so.

And they did, but that wasn't clear till waking
without their voices was only habit fixed
as the grinding of coffee, glance
at a window to check the weather.

But what if I take the final cup with me
to a porch where full-leaved maples are still
in bright and gathering warmth, to sit as if
I have entered a tree house, the one I wanted?

I have it now, and when the first
breeze of morning churns the light
and the only voices come from rooms
in a neighboring home, am I so far
from where I ever was? I woke
to something I could not prove was there
in all the hours that came before,
never the faded green of memory.

VICTORIA KELLY

To My Husband, Flying over Afghanistan

a cento

The pilot alone knows[1]
the chill of closed eyelids[2]
in the glaring white gap;[3]
the wired minefield;[4]
the stars in active orbit.[5]
And all is from wreck, here, there —[6]
the hot black dunes in the air.[7]

Now I am safe in the deep V of a weekday;[8]
how fibrous and incidental it all seems —[9]
the Avon lady trekking door to door,[10]
the paper sacks stuffed full of oranges,[11]
obscenely jewel-toned[12]
while the whole cathedral crashes at your back.[13]

---

[1] Andrew Joron, "Spine to Spin, Spoke to Speak"
[2] Marina Tsvetaeva, "Poems for Blok, 1" trans. Ilya Kaminsky & Jean Valentine
[3] Medbh McGuckian, "Painting by Moonlight"
[4] Ciaran Carson, "Let Us Go Then"
[5] Marie Ponsot, "Imagining Starry"
[6] Gerard Manley Hopkins, "The Times Are Nightfall…"
[7] Henri Cole, "Green Shade"
[8] Rachel Zucker, "After Baby After Baby"
[9] Sarah Gambito, "Holiday"
[10] David Trinidad, "9773 Comanche Ave."
[11] Shin Yu Pai, "Six Persimmons"
[12] Joyelle McSweeney, "A Peacock in Spring"
[13] Kamau Brathwaite, "Mesongs"

LeRoy N. Sorenson

Ghosts at Craigville

The road from Superior runs a hard
fifty miles to shanty Craigville
where eight bars and two whorehouses
once served a thousand men, most of them

one good winter from hell. Tonight fallen
shacks are pallid—small ones for loggers,
two-story ones for excess whores. Ruts
run from one building to another.

It's the kind of place where each
man lived the same life, told the same
stories. Bitter luck and ugly women
the norm. On crystal nights, wraiths

climb out of thin graves, make their way
to greener places. The sun burns them
hollow at sunrise. Some legacies never
end—the brutal way men crack

their backs with work, the passing years
thick with common derelicts.
Depletion drove loggers south and west
to gold fever and hardscrabble graves.

Those left behind stayed unloved,
yearned to return wide-eyed
to the motherland. Hunger
for women turned horizons
soft red, such longing ran down

roads mapped by an ill hand. No one
here could weep when it mattered,
their pale days gruel, above them stars—
raw as cut pine—fell away in every direction.

Denise Bergman

Alaska: Turnagain Bay

❖ Mt. Hope Trail

I want to say *Turnagain* over and over
until the skin falls off and bone comes to light

like the word *towel* (beach bath hand)
unraveled from terry and cloth to thread and bare
when we repeated it 200 times to see if the sound

the sometimes one, sometimes two syllables
could still wipe wet off dry

I want to, but focus instead on the steep dirt trail
rising

❖ The Overlook

Panting in thin air

the chant of bearbells untied
from backpack straps now a haphazard
clanking in our hands

Coming down, we lose footing, drop
into a bruising slide,
steer between boulders and sharp rocks
trying to keep our heads
off the ground

❖ Bore Tide

All that, to see the full face
of this mud-slathered bay, crown to mouth

its tongue
caught in the Pacific's icy throat—
no lapping rippling
hint of a mammoth tide

From above, time spreads in a wide brown wash
bending and waiting

but at the bank, each hour is a tease,
a temptation, irresistible—
like stepping into quicksand

expecting to step out

❖ Why "Turnagain"

Not because a bare river bottom
will in a flash be blanketed
by a six-foot cover of beluga and fish

not because a twelve-knot rolling wall
gives way

but because once a sea captain mapping his world
arrived at the gate too late

and had to turn his ship around
again

MARGE PIERCY

Tsunami

I try to imagine the people
after the rumble of the earthquake,
waiting, seeing it far off,
Was it like a mountain rushing toward them?

I too have stood and watched catastrophe
sweep toward me with nowhere to go
out of its path, too high, too wide
to run from. I have stood with a strange
weak smile, my heart caught on a barbed hook,
my breath opening in my chest
like a straight razor,
and felt the world crash down.

Roi J. Tamkin, *Water Abstract*, photograph

All fall down

Fall has burned itself out.
Now the gray ashen skies
and dun earth of November.
Color deserts us with migrating
geese in the sky like constellations.

The flowers are crisp, their
leaves sere. Already
the pesky chipmunks who take
one bite from each tomato
have gone to sleep.

Underfoot the leaves
blanched to torn paper bags
turn sodden with rain. Night
flows over day like ink
spreading into a blotter.

Our pole tilts into darkness.
The woods smell of decay.
The foxes are hungry. Soon
cold will seal us into our houses
to await the long snow.

Angela Patten

The Weather in Toronto, Winter 2007

What part of Canada are ye from,
the security guard in Belfast asks politely
as we step out of the car at the college gate.

Vermont, I say, in the U.S. But I'm Irish
born and raised, I hasten to add as I ladle out
an extra dollop of my Dublin accent.

But it says here ye are Canadian, he insists,
tapping his finger on his official memo.
Later someone mentions a grand wee holiday

in Niagara Falls, a daughter in Alberta,
a weather bulletin that says it's snowing in Toronto.
When they ask what took you out to Canada

in the first place I don't bother to defend myself,
shamed by the name of my old neighborhood
though it's three decades since I left home

and no one remembers the seedy history of my street
now the houses have changed hands
and people have money in their pockets.

Next day our driver gives us "the terror tour"
of Belfast—the Europa Hotel bombed 37 times,
the train station rebuilt from scratch.

Here's where the minister was shot. Here's the corner
where I saw a man lying dead in a pool of blood.
Nothing to worry about now. Not a wee bother.

Everyone here is happy to forget that history
ever happened. So why am I still lugging mine around
as if it was written on my forehead

like the mark of Cain or a terrorist slogan
dripping red paint down a rickety barricade—
part feeble fortification, part belligerent defense.

JEFFERSON HARRIS

The Elephant Seals

Imagine a sweet potato
the size of a truck.
Now imagine twenty such sweet potatoes
washed up on the beach at San Simeon.

The elephant seals are visiting, and the handout
given us by the nice volunteer informs us
that this is their season for "catastrophic molting."
It doesn't look catastrophic. It looks like
the world's deadest party, an array
of pharaonic bolsters, flung on the sand.

We watch from the bluffs,
in fascination: their shapelessness!
Which end is which? And what are they for?
And what do they do? Besides reproduce
(how?) and be huge? They seem at once
dangerous and helpless, inspiring
a kind of tenderness . . . .

One of them rears up, barks, then collapses.
Two or three are flinging sand about,
while one lifts a flipper aloft,
as if it held a martini . . . .

We get back in our cars, amused and thrilled
that such creatures exist, amazed
by these beings who sleep so much, like us,
and weigh so much, and are sometimes belligerent
though more often inert, and seem, like us,
to have no certain purpose, except to undergo
their catastrophic molting
and hunch their way back
to the ocean.

The Cliffs Beyond Akaroa

The seal sleeps underwater.
She rises in sleep to breathe.

I've been sleeping a long time
under the wide sea of the sky.

Over a reef on the continental
shelf, one wave has traveled

all my life but I don't know
which one. When I go flying

through foam, I try to guess
which of the waves is the lost

messenger and which crest
hides the missing message.

Above me, up on the steep
sea cliffs, tiny sheep dream

of the sheep station dogs,
those alarming white teeth.

Brad Johnson

The Birds

Like an angel placed last on a Christmas tree
a hummingbird perched atop
the undressed mountain ash in her backyard
where the black bear stood on its tip-toes
to topple the birdfeeder last Easter.

The hummingbird stared at my aunt
standing at her kitchen window
with her morning espresso and wool socks
worn at the toes. She'd never seen
a hummingbird this late in Seattle's December
and never seen one sit still like that.
The hummingbird was smaller than an infant's foot,
so small it drew no shadow.

Out back where Grandma chopped the birch down
but kept the stump for bird feed, she watched
a pileated woodpecker attack
the bark as though the bark approached
its eggs nesting in the tree's cavity.
It was wet-tire black with a wild red crown
and as big as a football deflating in the basement.
Its eyes wide, staring at all of Ashtabula at once.

Global warming must have affected
migration patterns. How else would Al Gore
explain the jay nestled in the bushy plumbago
behind my house fifty miles north of Miami?
It shakes its baby-blue plumage to get
my attention then points its crest toward heaven.

My aunt thinks this is Uncle Jay
communicating to us, talking
across the divide, saying hello
and good-bye and *I won't forget you
if you don't forget me.* Saying *I'm all around.
Open your eyes. Remember.*

I think it sucks he's missing all these birds.
He would have loved them.

Susan Cohen

Lucky Dog

My family bragged during my childhood
        that we owned a dog who smiled.
Mutt of memory, spring-loaded, black-coated,
        when I whistled she came bouncing.

Sometimes she arrived unbidden,
        all unleashed delight. She'd track me
to the school yard, leap to lick my chin,
        knock me flat onto the blacktop.

Suburban evenings on my bike,
        I heard neighbors calling. Their dogs
never came. We had our lucky dog,
        they had sour marriages, dour jobs,

common cancers no one named
        with children present. At the time,
I didn't wonder if our lucky mutt
        was one-part hound, some-part

myth like so much that I was taught
        of happy-ever-after. I just knew
she made me nervous when she pitched
        into my ribs. Already, living

seemed more complex than promised,
        affections excitable and fluid
as a high-voltage tail that sometimes whipped
        across bare legs and stung.

I'd done nothing to deserve
        her generous tongue that slopped
its unrelenting happiness on me, so
        maybe I didn't trust in her,

not fully, not even then.

        That lavish, bounding luck.

That doggy grin.

Monica Wendel

"Wikileaks Reveals That Military Contractors Have Not Lost Their Taste For Child Prostitutes"

—headline from www.huffingtonpost.com, December 8th, 2010

Two women say Julian Assange raped them.
Diplomatic cables say contractors in Afghanistan bought boys
for one night or longer. Julian, I can't root for you
while Bradley's alone in the brig. But you're also our best bet.
As for the hackers who took down Visa and MasterCard and PayPal—
I wish it was easier to know what to build.
Like how to make a government without violence,
and which crops besides opium grow in such a harsh climate.
I wish the hackers had found how to reach those boys now,
the ones who danced, veiled, one-named, vague except for this detail:
oldest, age 15; youngest, age 8.

DWAYNE THORPE

Noon Whistle

Does it still go off every day
wailing like an air-raid siren
to let grandmother know grandfather
is right now walking away from the worksite
so she had better take the bowl of cucumber slices
and chopped scallions floating in vinegar water
out of the icebox, put the plate of cold chicken
on the table along with pickled beets
and the bread baked this morning
before the sun was properly above the horizon?

And does everyone still pause where they are:
sidewalk, lumber yard, the Duckwalls glass door,
the loading dock at the icehouse
where kids sit kicking their heels and sucking ice slivers,
the post office bench where the Spit and Whittle Club
stop their jaws to listen in unison
while the whistle sinks and finally dies
to resume the push toward deep night
when the porch light at Doctor Schnoblen's house
is turned off and the streets release their breath?

Or if that sound is stilled, what reminds us
that we stand on a great ball rolling
toward the edge where everything drops away?

Tara Taylor

Something Else

A Response to Jack Gilbert's Disgust for Simile

Nothing is only what it is —
the Vidalia onion
sliced to bloom
on the bamboo
cutting board
looks like my little sister's
tulle ballet tutu
discarded in a bunch
on the hardwood floor.

A sashimi salmon rose —
cut of raw meat
fashioned on the plate —
is like the soft floret of cancer,
opening on the vine
of her throat,
the gun-metal shimmer
of petaled tissue
we clutch between chopsticks and chew.

How can anyone not
need simile —
the way it designs
a sweet vegetable
into the memory
or arranges disease
as a simple spring bouquet.

Haven't you ever asked
the obvious —
what does it look like I'm doing? —
and hoped for a bit of poetry?
How else can I say this?
Like a person in a photo of a waterfall
we need them for scale,
to show immensity.

Tara Taylor

Over dinner, I tell my sister
not to worry about
her CT scan next week.
The coffin tunnel, she calls it.
Think of the machine as a giant
Life Saver—that's what it
looks like, peppermint flavor.
You'll wait inside—
this ring-shaped lifebuoy—
eyes closed, teeth clenched,
you'll think of something else.

Mark Weiss, photograph

Handloom Fabrics

I skirted the tables, high as my head, flanking my mother. She would give the selvage a tug, and I could hear the bolts thump against the cutting table like a giant's heart. Stitching for us. Stitching us. I learned metaphors of cloth from her and the telling edge of a repeat. Now, I finger my bolt. Leather shears maybe? Sharp enough to cut muscle,

cut bone, scissor blades thick and mirrored. I know to measure it. No second chances after the first cut. No seconds. Can the little one do without me for short stints? Can the big one? How will they display the pain of this alteration? What will break inside them? What will remain? What will soften these agonies? My hands are clumsy now, our weft

ugly, clashing and random, keen to be abandoned. I know to measure. I wait until my breath scuttles past, watching its back. I wait until sleep leaves me, and my kidneys weep and spots blot my flawless skin. I wait until my small mother looms to say, "You *tell* the doctor she needs to be seen *today*," until the doctor says, "like a POW," my body

bowing low, bowing out. But mostly I hear no finished cloth for us, only thread. Spools and spools for all the ages the girls still reach for, and how will I embrace the broken ends, the meals I won't fix for us, baby teeth I may never palm, the lost pass of my hand over their brows, my way to end each day? I choose death over these unlivable risks,

tiptoe out in freezing temperatures, in panties, holding a phone, and curl in their sandbox. I call a friend to say good-bye. Then lie, on fire, unspooling.   Now   exaltation
as I cut what tumbles from the splendid reel, deciding to claim the truth of the turns, to mend again, to see our slubs and stains dear in the blades.

JOHN SUROWIECKI

D.D. (Elegy for a Copywriter)

He had no use for metaphors:
either a thing was what it was or it wasn't.
You couldn't linger over a phrase either.
If it was catchy, fine, if not, that was fine, too,
so long as it moved someone from stupor to sale,
a set of directions, a map, forged by research:
who could possibly lose their way?

Yet none of us doubted that the leaves
dropping from the sky were our hearts,
shriveled and desiccated and brown,
or that the crow's barks were our unlovely
inadequate words or that the moth
stirring on the red church door was a soul,
no doubt his and no doubt lost.

From the collection of the Managing Editor, photograph

John Surowiecki

A.B. (Four Last Songs)

Dying is just as I composed it.
           — Richard Strauss

1. Spring

Words come easily to her, dear
ciotka,* the overlooked flower,
the voice above the factory din.
She tap-tap-taps at the thickness
in her lungs, explains the merits
of a productive cough, doesn't complain
when it's difficult to breathe
or impossible to eat.

2. September

She doesn't know what month it is,
just that it's not quite summer anymore
and summer's not what it used to be.
There's a chill in the air to and from
dialysis and she hears children again
in the schoolyard. A nurse says the darkness
arrives earlier this time of year and she says
pretty soon it'll be there from the start.

3. Going to Sleep

She says there's no good reason
why she shouldn't light up a Pall Mall
or sip a Manhattan before bed,
C.C. and Cinzano *Rosso,* even-steven,
with a dash of bitters at the end
and served neat in a glass so elegant
it sings: and of course a maraschino
as its throbbing scarlet heart.

168

4. At Sunset

I tell her corny jokes but it's troubling
to hear her laugh, a muffled sound
from another world where the light
is always orange and concluding,
just as she had pictured it: potato salad
and starred hot dogs, sweet yellow corn,
games of setback, golden highballs clinking
and children somewhere far away.

*Ciotka means aunt in Polish

Mark Weiss, photograph

John Surowiecki

Making My Sister Laugh

When she asks for money I
take out a five and make it fly.
She always gets the joke and
remembers for a little while
at least what it was like before
the homes and mental hospitals,
the FBI agents and the death
camps behind the Stop&Shop,
before the baby, hers for an hour,
and the bus rides to see people
who always lived somewhere else,
before all that—to a time when
we shared the Sunday comics
on a rectangle of sunlit carpet:
suddenly there were bills to pay
and anniversary gifts to buy and
out of Dagwood's wallet or Hi's
pocket escaped winged fins or,
funnier still, because we didn't
know how it got there or what
it meant, a moth, its dark cozy
moth life interrupted, pulling
dotted lines of flight into a pale
blue sky, itself only pale blue dots.

Simon Perchik

*

Gasping on air and salt
and though you can hear the soup cool
an ocean deep inside the Earth

is bubbling under your skull
exhausted—it's natural you wait
for the soup to grieve

louder and louder as if your arms
were coming too close—wave after wave
you scatter more salt

and across the bowl
that smells from rain in the beginning
—it's expected that you have this appetite

for reef, for a sea with a bone in its mouth
and along the coast the dead fingers
the dead lips listening for yours

tired from struggling—only soup
and even then a wooden chair
so nothing is forgotten.

CHRISTOPHER ROBINSON

Cicatrix

On the roof, I smoke a cigar and drink Chianti
from the bottle. This is the hour of molten window
and near collision, the hour of light wind where the sky
blends with the pool of transmission fluid
and the rusted chain-link across the street.
Through a vent-pipe, I hear a man cough in a room
below—this is the hour of half-conversation, comings
and goings forgotten, when the tip of a cigar is the same
color as the sun on the roofer's tools in the pickup
truck, the shingle hatchet and brackets of a man
who now draws out an uncertain note on his bow
as his violin rosin glows on his windowsill
the color of the sky. The only sounds slip above
the surface of this hour like the backs of fish.

No bodies should remain untouched: that's why
I burned my hands with cigarettes. To speak
in another language, untainted by association
(key, lock; smoke, ash), the language of things
(mouth, hole; eye, hole), the language of certain things
at certain times—How else could I speak to you
than in the hour of dog-walkers and observers
of observers, the hour of reading and rereading the space
between words on the cooling roof? I cannot touch you
with language, I know, but let the sun, touched
orange-red, spread thin in the hour of slow,
slow exhalation and eavesdropping moon, let us
share a silence, let us be indistinguishable for an hour.

E. Louise Beach

Ombra mai fù

Never was a shade more perfect.

The night is soft and bright
and without wind
ghost-white
the plane tree teases
her dreams its green
fronds *tenere e belle*
she would tarry beneath
its leaves lap robe
on her knees
Mother listens
to the famed aria
from Händel's *Xerxes*
sung by her brother
dead three years
the stairs are steep
and sleep is heavy
Wolf Moon, Snow Moon,
Old Moon
present in the room
his pure tenor
tuxedo and thinning hair
and she is withered
leafless
bereft of words
though once loveliest
of sycamores soaring
from black alluvium
at river's edge

Vocalise

Sabotaged by a mind
(her own)
she has forgotten the sad,
sacked words
(no sense, no *parole*);
sings vowels
(her only attendant
the appellant wind).
Falling, she falls.
I gather Mom up in my shawl
and take her home.
Where were you going to, Darkling?

She adapts her tunes from
melodies for bereavement,
old lullabies
(*lully lully*)
and glorious hymns;
croons incidental airs
(*ciel et vent*)
that float overhead,
then disperse
(!)
sudden as starlings
swirling above the shriven stooks.

Mekeel McBride

Gazebo

If I had to choose one—and let the rest go—
gazebo's the word I'd take for my own,
the art deco elegance of z, the easy work it does

connecting vowels; *steady, fixed attention*,
from *videbo, I shall see*; free-standing,
roofed structure,

usually open at the sides,
the secret side of Victoriana, insisting
on a structure merely for summer pleasure.

I say *gazebo* to myself especially
in the middle of winter; it helps to hear
those insouciant syllables,

a little like the white-throated sparrow's
early arrival in February, months too early
but ready anyway. A word that smells of cut

grass, latticework, cake and rain. You were
married. I wasn't. And we were crazy
drunk. Well past three a.m., the park empty

and in the dark gazebo we kissed as if
those kisses were going to keep
the world alive. Years later, alone,

you died of heart attack, weren't found
for days. One way to remember is to keep
saying it, effortless guest, snow ghost, *gazebo* . . .

What If

        someone had noticed you were a child, too small to hold
together the whole world with one small voice. What if you had been allowed
to roller skate have friends get ice cream after school go to school fall
asleep while someone sang *to you*?
        Why didn't anyone try to stop you
from vanishing piece by piece so much plastic surgery even a marionette
would have been ashamed to call you brother?
        We *wanted* that glove of diamonds we said diamonds even though we knew better to touch
star-high shine into every single one of our boring days, wanted you to sing us
smack into the middle of that love-soaked stage.
        Beaten like a dog, trained like a dog, but never
loved the way a dog can sometimes be loved. We pulled off your clothes, kissed
you, screamed for you, chased and trampled you. Your houses got bigger your
bones got more brittle you stopped eating sleeping even stopped singing.
        We started laughing even
though we said we loved you but really meaning we were so
over you, so much better than you, had *always* been better than you, little splinter
boy dressed in spider silk, your nose, your hair falling off,
we could not stop laughing.
        But it's all right, you've died and some mag said, *the true
riches of his afterlife can now begin*, as if mission accomplished you might do a
Lazarus Houdini hip-hop riff and rise into this newfound wealth, love and money
a new body of grace and blaze. Not that it matters but I can't even begin
        to tell you
how sorry I am and when the extravaganza of your memorial settles its glitter
blizzard into television, I'll be outside, maybe, in the trees, in the rain because
that's all it does here lately is rain, singing a lullaby and no one will hear except
for me and in the lost green silence, I hope
        you.

Enough

"How do you say, 'I've had enough' in English?" Astrid asks. I swirl another bread cube in fondue and laugh. We're both over fifty and shouldn't be anywhere near this much cheese.

"It's a problem in German," she continues. "There's really no way. *Ich bin Sat* sounds impolite, like you're stuffed."

"What about just saying *Ich habe Genug*?" *I've had enough.*

"No." She shakes her head. "That sounds like it didn't taste very good."

Ich habe Genug. I sit with my two sisters on a sunny May afternoon, weeping as we listen to Bach's cantata, baritone solo and bassoon mingling with the last of Mother's presence in the emptied apartment.

When her cardiologist said there was nothing he could do for her, she stopped eating. Except for the week before she died when I took her to Rachel's Bread. She ate a whole sandwich: havarti and greens on cranberry wheatberry sourdough.

"That tasted good," she said when she was finished. *Es hat sehr gut geschmeckt.*

Flight Patterns

At the edge of the marsh the redwing blackbirds
swoop onto the tips of cattails
pu-twee, churee, chit-chit-chit.

I wheel your chair into a patch of sun
over the boggy dips and tussocks of bluestem
so you're not shaken

snatch up the peach mohair stole to warm you
against the raw air. From your apartment window
you used to watch the swans glide in the artificial pond

wings clipped so they would stay.
I crouch at the edge of the marsh with my notebook.
The dried stems sway as the birds take flight.

From the collection of the Managing Editor, photograph

JadeDragon_77

If I hear the song in my running dreams, then I fly, or I lift the ceiling and take off through it. When I hear the song awake I know something is about to happen. My eardrums tickle. Suddenly the sleep music stops and the door opens part-way. Here in the dormitory at Crippled Children's Hospital and School there aren't any locks. It's Saturday and I'm in my nightgown. I sit up on my bed and dig my fingers into my calves that feel spongy, not like the strong legs I used to tapdance with.

"Is Rose about?" a guy's voice asks. "I'm her brother Wiley." He pushes the door in all the way and stands next to Rose's desk rubbing his hands together. The fringes of his suede jacket look frozen as icicles. He's tall.

"She's in the hospital with chicken pox," I say, reaching for my wheelchair parked beside the bed. "Quarantined."

The hospital is in another building separate from the school dormitory. Rose has multiple sclerosis and we've roomed together since the eighth grade and now we're juniors. There's not a kinder or smarter person on Earth. It must have been because she was born on the Reservation that she'd missed her chickenpox vaccination.

"You're Jana, right?" he asks the air. Unless he comes in farther he can't see me.

"Wrong. I'm 77." I glance over at the empty bed across the stretch of gray-pink flecked linoleum where strewn clothes look like they're trying to run away. The floor seeps heat no matter how cold the room is. Like summer in Destoroyah, not winter Sioux Falls, South Dakota. My alter ego is JadeDragon_77, a female warrior from the Temple of Godzilla. I love Godzilla movies.

He chuckles, walking deeper into the messy room and finding out for himself Rose isn't there. Snow is melting from his silver-tipped boots, drooling puddles on the linoleum. He glances in my direction and then does a double-take. His mouth falls open. I'm wearing a red sleeveless nightgown that pictures a smiling cat and the words Hello Kitty. It doesn't look that bad. It hits just below the knee. His jacket's sleeves smell like they're thawing. Rose told everyone for months he was coming. Everyone knows how proud she is of her brother graduating from law school at the University of Wyoming. Big shit Wiley who didn't show up for Thanksgiving or Christmas or her birthday. They forgive him for everything because his fiancée was abducted from a mall parking lot and killed. But that was years ago. Wiley is the first Barking Moose to finish high school, college, and then law school. By this time next year Rose will be the second Barking Moose to graduate from high school. I'm usually the smartest person in every gathering. That's why I know better than to put in hours studying. Why I read only what interests me. They scraped Crippled Children's faculty from the bottom of South Dakota's pedagogic barrel: geriatric substitute teachers and PE coaches dismissed for cause from regular schools.

"Well, aren't you going to ask how your sister is?" I say.

He pulls the tie out of his ponytail and shakes his hair free, like a black horse stumbling up rimrock and finding its footing, then he bands it back up again. His eyes are the same as Rose's, without pupils or irises, just solid black suns that could heat whatever they looked at. Like the strike and slam of black flint.

"How is she?" he asks, craning to look at the pyramid of Coke cans taped together to resemble the great pyramid in the Valley of Kings. Then he seems to be studying me. "Rose told me about you." His glance of a second ago turns into a staring contest. Who will blink first? "My sister said you were very pretty."

I wonder how he heard that since he never visits or calls. I drop my legs over the side of the bed. My nightie bunches up and I notice him noticing the dirty bottoms of my feet. Check out the linoleum floor if you wonder why. I need to transfer into my chair but that's my business how I get from bed into my wheelchair. I don't want to do it in front of him. He slips his hand into his jean pocket and digs for keys. "Can you show me where the hospital is?" he asks. My cheeks burn and I tell him I have to get dressed first. He can ask one of the aides to show him or he can wait outside in the hall.

❊ ❊ ❊

After I've changed into my JadeDragon_77 t-shirt and jeans I roll out barefoot into the hall and find Wiley waiting. He knows from being around his sister how to walk alongside a wheelchair girl and not push in a bum's rush. I lead him through the tunnel that intersects the physical therapy rooms and the hospital facility.

There's the click of Canadian canes, the thump of crutches. The parallel bars they torture you on. As long as you can walk, no matter if you do it like a crab, you're better off. No thank you. I sit in a wheelchair and move myself along with my feet. I hate wearing socks and shoes, but in winter when I go outside I compromise and wear clogs.

"Hey 77," the physical therapist Wesley Snobel says to me, smiling. He seems to be on his way to the soda machine in the hospital lobby. He's a large-bodied, square-headed man with brown eyes and frame glasses; a goofy grin takes up most of his lower face. "I missed you in Wednesday's gym class." Well, I sure didn't miss him or the class where they make gimps play Ping-Pong or badminton. The A.B. aides have to run all over for the balls and birdies. "Remember, 77, if you want to graduate with your class, physical education is mandatory."

I roll my eyes.

He gives Wiley Barking Moose the once over and waits expecting me to make an introduction. If he expects that he'll have a long wait. I roll into the hospital lobby, where Eleanor Peglog sits at reception. Wiley follows. Wesley Snobel must put two and two together and at least come up with five. "Oh, you must be one of Rose's relatives," he lights up, "but sorry you won't be able to see her. Chicken pox is a communicable disease. There are students around here who might not survive a bout of it." Then he gives me a meaningful look and addresses himself again to Wiley. "Mrs. Peglog will tell you the same thing. We take extreme care. Our students come first. And, 77, put some shoes on."

We enter the butter-pat-sized lobby of the twenty-bed hospital that adjoins Crippled Children's School. Mrs. Peglog, wearing her purple eyeshadow and candy-striper uniform, queens the security desk. She reminds me a little of my other icon, Tammy Faye Baker of the PTL (Praise the Lord) Club. Wiley explains who he is and how he wants to visit his sister.

"No can do, Mister Barking Moose. Rose is in quarantine. Absolutely no visitors," she says, batting her eyelashes like mascara-drenched spiders. I think of Godzilla vs. Hedorah. The alien Hedorah evolves into an amphibian and his gigantic tongue licks the pollution from the air. He fattens on plastic bags and sludge. Mrs. Peglog and Wesley Snobel remind me of the poisonous emissions of Hedorah.

"What a drag," Wiley says, reaching into his jacket for gum, and offers me something fruit-striped. I fold a stick into my mouth. "I'm sorry for waking you," he apologizes, then takes hold of the grip bars on my chair and pushes me down the hall, hurtling me along. I thought he knew better. You couldn't count on people. Like Rose couldn't count on Wiley. The only thing you can do with people is trick them. When we reach the elevator he lets go of my chair. From the side his jaw juts. Like the photograph of Crazy Horse on his pinto, his nose high and sharp.

"Would you mind taking me to Dunkin' Donuts?" I ask. "I like the coffee there with real cream." That is what they cleared off the Cheyenne and Crow and Oglala Sioux to build.

The elevator opens and he pushes me inside. He hesitates. "I don't know where Dunkin' Donuts is. And you'd have to put socks on and get a coat if I said yes. Really, I need to get going."

"Well, where are you going?"

He looks like he's deciding whether to answer. The horses are stumbling on the rimrock. "Near Pipestone. I have a cabin there. I'm going to hole up for a month and study for my bar exam."

"You mean if they'd let us in to see Rose this is all the longer you would stay? She thought she could count on you for Thanksgiving." I push the hair out of my face. "I need to get going too. But I never get to go anywhere!"

He takes the gum out of his mouth and balls it into the wrapper and looks for a wastebasket, then apologizes for being in a hurry. "How old are you?"

I shrug. "How old are you?"

"Twenty-six," he answers.

"I'm sixteen."

His eyes spark, but deep inside like flints striking. Like you could fall a long way into them before you hit bottom. "You have to get your coat, 77. It's about ten degrees outside."

Sixteen is the age of consent in South Dakota. At sixteen you can drop out of high school. You can marry. I don't bother with the sign-out sheet next to the front door.

※ ※ ※

Wind blows across the crusts of old snow in the parking lot.

All the dirty snow reminds me of how my eyes roll back when I'm asleep, and because the muscles in my lids don't work properly they can't close all the way. It is how the dead sleep and I imagine when Godzilla dozes his eyes roll back like milk buckets. Wiley pushes me in my wheelchair to the oldest Ford pickup in the lot. The hood must have been replaced because it's yellow while the rest of the truck is a deep indigo blue. The fenders and grill and headlight caps shine. I like that. How people care for their things means a great deal to me. He opens the passenger's door, then lifts me into the cab. I don't feel him brace himself or stagger. I smell clay and scrub-brush. In the side mirror I watch him roll my chair around to the back and lift it. He doesn't slam or bounce it. Two feathers hang from Wiley's rearview, one black, one grayish white. Instead of butts there are jellybeans in the ashtray. There's more smell of sage.

"Take a left on red, and Dunkin' Donuts is on the right." I tell him. We pull into the only available space between a police cruiser and a tow truck. A cop sits in the passenger's seat and you can hear the radio crackling. Another policeman lumbers out of Dunkin' Donuts. He's bald as a doorknob and carrying two coffees and a donut bag along with his fat-ass citation book. His stomach wraps over his belt while he gives Wiley the twice-over. The cop's eyebrows lift as he hurries over to circle around the blue Ford checking out its yellow hood, the University of Wyoming sticker, and finally the bed of the truck. Spotting the wheelchair, he really looks. This time at me. I pretend to pick my nose. "Geez, that's quite a sight!" he bellows to his partner. Wiley grips the steering wheel, the nerve in his cheek twitching. The clouds have turned to dirty soapsuds and dishrags. I tell Wiley I changed my mind about going inside. I don't want the cops to bother him. The police in South Dakota don't like Indians. You'd think it was their people who got corralled into reservations.

"Okay," Wiley says, tapping the dash, "so if you don't want coffee I'll take you back to Crippled Children's." His fingers remind me of creek water and smoke since they don't stay long in one place. But his eyes do. They keep looking at my face. I want him to think I'm pretty. People always tell me I am, but who believes them? They patronize.

I stare back at him. "You promised you'd take me for a ride.

Are you really going to Pipestone?"

He watches the cop taking down his license tags. "No, Crooks, South Dakota. If you blink you miss it."

"I want to go too."

"I can't take you out on the highway," he says.

"Yes, you can. How far is it from here?"

"An hour."

"You mean you can't take an hour out of your life to drive me there and take another hour to drive me back? Rose would want me to see your house so I can tell her about it. I bet your sister never visited it." I look down at my hands, and then up at him as if beseeching, although JadeDragon_77 would never beseech or beg or say the bad word *please*. The real bad word is *MD*. Muscular Dystrophy. Onset in childhood. Muscle wasting. Shortened life span. Loss of ability to walk. The bad word is Father. Who suffered from invisible MD, never telling my mother until he had to—the day I was diagnosed.

Wiley makes a turn in the seat, reaches into the ashtray for the red jellybeans, offers me some. I take two. I like him. "Listen, I usually don't carry passengers. I brought you here because it's not far."

"Why? Because you were driving around while your fiancée got killed?"

There's a flash of lightning in his face, a clenching of his jaw. "I guess my sister told you that."

"No, she didn't," I lie. "I read minds."

"So you're clairvoyant?"

"I am."

But I'm not and Rose didn't tell me much because that subject is off-limits. I only know Wiley gave a friend of his a ride somewhere and when his fiancée finished shopping he wasn't there to pick her up. That's when the man stepped out of his nothingness and pulled his knife and forced her into his car.

❊ ❊ ❊

The snow is about to fall into the noon twilight and stir up the wind. The sky holds its breath. I feel free in Wiley's truck, being this high up, the wheels under me. I like how he drives, his left boot stepping on the clutch, his right hand shifting. First, second, third gear. He never pops the clutch. I show Wiley a photograph of my family. It just happened to be forgotten in my jacket pocket. We're stopped at a red light in a tiny town. A grain elevator and a beer tavern, a four-way stop sign. There's my parents. My black-haired brothers look almost as Lakota as Wiley except they're seated on a couch surrounded by pale blue carpet instead of stuck in a camper heated by propane. "Was this you?" he asks, pointing to the unsmiling girl sitting on the carpet. "You were a prim little thing." I chuckle.

The little town disappears and we drive into more country. The early afternoon light is sinking into the ramshackle fields. Soon dark will creep up from the ditches. Winter light is more vivid than summer light. It knows when it's about to die. The heater doesn't work well and the windshield keeps icing over. The temperature must be dropping.

"How many kids are you eventually going to have, Wiley?" I ask.

"Zero," he tells me and then pulls over onto the shoulder and gets out with the ice scraper to clear the windshield wipers. His breath is white when he jumps back inside. "Remember, I almost was married," he says, his strong jaw clenching, "and I won't go near that again." He owns a little house in the woods where South Dakota almost becomes Minnesota. He and his fiancée, Liliane, bought it when they were in college with leftover student aid money. It was an eyesore, but they'd worked hard fixing it up. They never lived in it together. His fiancée was killed the summer after their junior year. At first he thought she'd come back, that she'd just forgotten herself and somehow disappeared. He hoped, prayed to his ancestors for Liliane to still be alive. Then police revealed that a man's face captured by mall security cameras the afternoon she vanished was of a recently paroled sex offender. Video showed the man lighting a new cigarette from the old one like the cigarette was his air and he had to keep one going to breathe. Joe Hawk. Age 40. His jerky hands, his entire body had a confused, startled look. Joe Hawk denied having anything to do with Liliane. There was no real evidence. The police questioned whether Liliane was even dead. Wiley drank too much after that. Then one day while driving his Toyota he was broadsided by a woman living in her car with her vodka bottle and her eighty-year-old mother. She'd barreled through the red light into him. "They were homeless. I wanted to hate them. I hated everyone for a while," he admitted. "But that crash woke me up. Hating only hurts the hater."

"Yesterday I hated my father, but most days I don't." When he asks me why I hate my father I shrug, changing the subject. "Does your gas gauge work? It says Empty. It has the whole time we've been driving. And the clock says 10:10. Is that the last time you bought gas?"

He laughs and I like his face even better. "Yes, it always reads Empty. We have plenty of gas to reach Crooks. There's an old guy who runs a gas station. I like to give him business."

If we run out of gas, that wouldn't be so bad. When I see the first snowflakes drifting down like torn Kleenex I scoot against the door and roll down the window to catch them. Cold soft. I taste it from my cupped hand. "Want some?" I ask him, extending my hand.

"You shouldn't be asking that of grown men, 77," he says, the laugh disappearing,

"You're putting on a disapproval face," I tell him. "Draggy teachers always wear them." I lean my head farther and farther out the window and wait for him to tell me to roll it up but he doesn't. I look into the side mirror wondering how my wheelchair is faring with cold falling through its spokes. The chair has powers. It doesn't exhale atomic fire like Godzilla, although its hide is tough and snakes can't swallow it. And it's like a horse too. The wheelchair wants to be cared for and remembers mistreatment. Here the cab's seat smells like brown leaves lying on damp earth streaked with clay. I roll the window up on my own.

"Your face is Lakota, you know." He keeps looking at me, even the angles of his cheeks look.

"What's it to you?" I say, feeling goosebumps in my stomach.

"It isn't anything to me. But you look like Liliane."

Like the dead girl who was native. I've always been told I look Indian by white people. But I don't, not really. Not my cheekbones or the color of my skin. I have brown almost black hair and brown, almond-shaped eyes. And I can't smile so I look solemn. Some of the kids think I'm stuck up. "Does your radio work?" I ask. It would be nice to watch the trees and fences go by and listen to music. The light might fade into the roofs of barns and the abandoned orchards in time to drums.

When he answers me his eyes are black snowflakes melting

in the windshield. "It does but I like to hear myself think. I like to hear the thoughts of whatever is around me." Then almost as an afterthought he adds, "It took a year before Liliane's body was found by a boy digging for arrowheads."

※ ※ ※

Her death stayed silent like those of goats and sheep and cows. Her bones marked by a hunting knife and teeth. The hunger of small animals. I'm wondering about Joe Hawk and what happened to him after Liliane's body was found. The kind of stuff Wiley thinks seems to have a good deal to do with either his fiancée or his bar examination and how he expects to practice as a legal aid lawyer. He studied on a scholarship set aside for a Lakota Sioux. He made his peace with Liliane's spirit. Do I know the Lakota have the shortest life expectancy of any peoples in the world? When native women go missing the authorities don't really look for them. Liliane would want him to help their tribe. He's going to pass the bar exam for her. That's one more reason he's going into the woods—to study and meditate. I'd like to make each moment I live in expand.

Is he trying to hear my thoughts? Probably not. He's not thinking about me at all. And why should he? I'm a kid. His sister's age. He's tolerating me like an older brother does. There's a funny light coming from the stubble poking through the old snow and from the farmhouses that look like no one has ever lived in them. I light a cigarette. A Virginia Slim or Virginia Slimes as I like to call them. They are the brand of cigarettes Godzilla smokes. I crack the window.

Wiley's head jerks to look at me, "What are you doing?"

"Relaxing."

"Put that thing out. That's death you've got in your mouth. Are you crazy?"

I toss the cigarette out, watching it spark behind the truck. I think he cares about me like a little sister. He might not let Rose smoke either.

"You're quite the rebel," Wiley remarks, lifting his eyes into the rearview. "Liliane was too." He reaches into his jellybean ashtray and chooses the black licorice ones. He tells me nothing happened to Joe Hawk because the trail went cold after a year.

The police even questioned him. Wiley took a lie detector test and passed. He took time off before law school to dig into the sex offender's past, following him around to bars and shopping malls, to rivers and fish-houses. He had to let it go. Joe Hawk was part Oglala but never lived on the Res. Instead his white mother took care of him and still does. Wiley came to understand the sex offense on Joe Hawk's record came from his having had relations at age seventeen with his fifteen-year-old girlfriend. The rest of his trouble came from drugs. If Joe Hawk didn't do it, whoever killed Liliane was still out there.

Wiley reaches for a bottle of water, offers me a swallow. I take the bottle, swigging. "Do you mind me asking why you can't walk?" he asks.

I cough on a mouthful of water and a black jellybean. "Sure, I mind. Why would you think I wouldn't?"

"Because you look tough. Mysterious. Like the trees."

I wanted to ask what Liliane was like but he spoiled it with the same old question. The one everyone asks, although I like being compared to trees.

"I've got muscular dystrophy," I say, pressing my thumb into the cold of the window. "My father gave it to me although I don't blame him."

※ ※ ※

It was me not smiling that finally woke Richard, my father, up. I remember being ten years old in my camel-colored pleated skirt seated on the floor with legs to the side, as if riding the carpet sidesaddle. The Siamese Sasha lies against my leg. For a moment the photographer focuses on me and the cat. He tells us we both have bewitching eyes. Ten is a peculiar age, awkward, but I had those long slanting lids and dark brown irises staring out so solemnly. A cat-girl. Behind me the stupid flocked Christmas tree and the blue stars and red satin-covered balls. Okay, let's all smile. Big smile on the count of three. "Cheese, say cheese," the photographer commanded. I could see him thinking he'd have to get the cat of a girl to smile, to stop staring at him with those slow river eyes; she knew he needed get to his next house, his next appointment. Just get her to smile, like her two brothers, Steve and Christian, honor society boys in cable-knit sweaters, like Sharon, the gaptoothed younger sister, grinning ear to ear. "Jana, would you look this way and say cheese." Maybe my eyes flashed, irritated because I was smiling, at least I thought I was. I could feel it in my cheeks and chin. He wanted me to show teeth. "Spaghetti, Jana, relax. Think spaghetti and say cheese." I was looking his way, and then I said cheese but the word didn't turn my mouth into white-teeth. My father, sitting on the couch next to my mother, looked at me. In that moment he knew I had it. Earlier I'd seen him trip going up the steps into the living room. His leg gave out, then he immediately righted himself. I tore that photograph of my Christmas family into many pieces; I tore up the fireplace burning its gas log, the eggnog and fruitcake, a can of Redi-Whip, the ruby-red goblets. I reminded my father of a Siamese cat too. I had the secret in me like he had it in him. I tore up the handsome father seated next to my fine-boned mother, who wore a turquoise skirt and cashmere sweater her lover had given her. I tore her up too. I tore up the tinsel tree with blue bulbs.

* * *

Crooks, South Dakota. Finally we're in Wiley's town, what there is of it. Chuck's Hideaway and the U.S. Post Office share space with a Happy Chef café. Snow is starting to blow sideways across the highway. We turn into Buck's Filling Station & Snacks where a haywagon collapses next to the storefront. The one Phillips 66 pump is fat and round and the sign says ADD $2 TO EVERY GALLON. Wiley gets out of the truck, walks with his arms straight down and close to his sides, his hands clenched. The wind takes the store's screen door and slams it.

I roll my window down when an old man shuffles out wearing a shabby brown cap with earflaps. "Sorry, partner, they retired me," he says. "Phillips 66 won't deliver gas. Nothing in the pump, Wiley." The old man's lip wrinkles, showing creases like a farmer's hands. "Maybe I've got one can of gas I can give you. I'll siphon it from my station wagon." Old Buck does his best but the gas in his car doesn't fill a quarter of the red can. Wiley thinks that might be enough to get us to his place, then he'll hitchhike to Pipestone and fill two cans. "You kids be careful," Buck says, holding onto Wiley's door. "There's a blizzard coming. It's about on top of us."

A blizzard. I'm thrilled. The wind blows even harder once

we're back out on the two-lane highway and rattles the truck. It takes both of Wiley's hands to keep the vehicle on the road. The snow gives off a peculiar yellow color. It pings against the truck. All at once, everything blurs. Goes white. A white-out, the clouds spewing snow. The wind vulture starts to sing. Wiley hits his high beams. "Okay, 77, you're my navigator. We're about a half-mile from the turnoff for my place. I can't see the road. If you spot the ditch getting close call out. We're running on fumes. Let's hope we make it."

Sure, let's hope.

※ ※ ※

In the blowing snow the telephone lines strung between poles start to swing. Like jumpropes. I was good in elementary school at double jump rope. Skip. Hop. I liked the sound of rope smacking the ground. Another blast of wind shakes the truck. The windows vibrate. Wiley works the clutch, shifts us into high gear, and tries to ride it out. I tried to ride it out too when I started to fall down in seventh grade. I kept getting up. Are you all right, Miss Genevieve asked. I didn't answer. Another windblast rocks us and the truck starts to sputter. We're going to try coasting. Gradually, we lose speed. We make the turn onto a gravel road. Barely. Then gravel catches the tires. Wiley steers us toward the shoulder. The truck is wounded. We stop.

"We're less than a quarter-mile from my place," Wiley says in a rushed voice. "We can't stay here. We'll freeze. I'm going to carry you." There's fear in his voice, something I haven't heard before. He'll carry me on his back. I can hang on, can't I? Sure, I can hang on, but it will be easier to push me. Just get my wheelchair out of the back. I can help with my feet. The wheels will stick in the snow. No, you have to take my wheelchair or else leave me here. "Look, your socks are so thin as to be nonexistent," he says. We argue. I don't want to be without my chair. If there's enough road I'll make it.

"That's not a warm coat. You're going to wear my hat." He buttons my suede jacket, and then he reaches behind the seat for a bag that holds old clothes. Stuff he donates to the Res. He ties a spare long-sleeved shirt around my neck like a muffler and pulls a stocking hat on my head. I watch him tie another shirt around his neck and put on gloves.

"Try to keep your head down when the wind hits." He shoulders his door open.

It takes all of him to keep it ajar and slide himself out. I think of Crazy Horse. A Sioux too. I strap my purse over my shoulder. I feel happy. Far away from the house where I grew up. I don't see Wiley until the passenger's door swings wide and he jams my wheelchair against the seat. Somehow I slide out and he catches me and I land in my chair. The bite of the wind takes hold. My next breath is pulled from my nose. JadeDragon_77, a female warrior from the Temple of Godzilla, arrives. He pushes me into the stinging needles. I pull with my feet while snow flies into my mouth, sticks its fingers up my nose. I almost can't breathe. The chair sticks, won't move. I try to help more with my feet, but they're far away. I kick at the snow. I can't feel my feet. The wheels of my chair keep getting stuck in the snow. He's shouting into the wind of white ravens. "Not much farther! Doing okay?"

※ ※ ※

I'm trembling like the day I couldn't climb the stairs to my tapdance class. More white ravens. I hear wings beating and in the snow are the steps to Mr. Sells's practice room. He lived in a big old Victorian house in Pierre with a flight of stairs, and then a curve and up another flight. Beautiful wooden banisters carved with ring-necked pheasants, the state bird. My mother signed me up for ballet and tap lessons. That was before the X-linked gene derailed my future. I had just seen my first Godzilla movie.

Another shock of wind. I can't see anything. I can hear Mr. Sells talking about living in Paris or Barcelona, how soon he wanted to fly away, migrate to a soulful alive city. Pierre was isolated. Backward. He filled his house with antiques and chairs you didn't dare sit in because the French Revolution was about to break out when they were built and the wood had rotted into green worms. And he had photographs of the most interesting woman in the world. Her face perched on the wall like a garishly feathered bird. Her eyes were mouths. Her lips looked as if glass had ripped them. She posed in a coat of leopard spots and walked two leopards on leashes. Mr. Sells wanted to live grand like that, but he'd studied dance at the University of South Dakota. He gave dance lessons in his mother's house. Her clutter everywhere except the practice room with its pristine floor.

The snow burns and in the wind Mrs. Sells's doilies and salt and pepper shakers tumble. I can't see. I don't know if we're moving, but I'm trying to help. My eyes tear and my lashes freeze together. Mr. Sells keeps calling from inside the wind. Gay and very nice, he's in his tap shoes on the hardwood floor buffed to a blond gloss. The snow hisses, "Slide leg forward, drop heel." Intermediate tap. Mostly white girls. I stand by the one Sioux girl who's been adopted by a wealthy couple. I stare at us in the mirror and see girls more alike than different. Then I'm at the bottom of the steps again. Class has already started. I grasp the banister to climb the stairs that a year ago I didn't have to think about. I shake, each step makes my legs quiver. Shaking, I hang on, and then lift my leg with my hands and set my foot on the next step. Mr. Sells has already closed the door; the taps are sliding over the floor, like tiny hammers, hitting, hitting.

"*77!*" someone shouts.

Last stretch. He carries me through the snow into the gingerbread house.

❊ ❊ ❊

Wiley's long fingers massage like they are soothing hungry spots. He's kneeling next to the couch and my feet are in his hands. My teeth chatter. He keeps rubbing my feet. I don't feel them. A candle is the only light and shadows left by other people creep over the ceiling. Wind howls. I still have feet. I just can't feel them, and then I do. He's looking over my head at the wind. The snow hitting the house sounds like rocks.

Wiley lets go of my feet. He stands. "This is what happens to a bad idea, *77*. It gets worse. I knew I shouldn't have brought you along."

Where is it? I don't see it. He didn't abandon my chair, did he? Please. I lift my head. My wheelchair is next to the couch. Safe. He walks into the next room, and comes back with blankets. He wraps me in one, covers me in another. I still feel the bitter cold. The candle's flame shivers.

"Can you feel your toes yet?" he asks, worried. "I've started a fire in the stove. I'm going to have to cut more wood to get us through the night. Then I'll make some tea." Smoke from burning wood fills the room. Through the haze the knotty pine walls look on. It feels like the dark eyes of deer are staring. Wiley's searching for a blanket to wrap himself in. He has to keep feeding the fire. "You could be frostbitten," he tells me when he returns.

I think about my feet in his hands.

He pulls a little table over and sets the cups down. There are fruits and vegetables painted on the pot. He seats himself in my wheelchair and we drink tea that tastes like rainwater. I know at this moment that I want him to love me. We stare at each other. Without saying anything we're playing the silence game. Who will look away first? The candle flickers in his face. A wick in each eye. "You're the first girl since Liliane in this house," he informs me, beckoning by not moving at all.

I can almost touch the little picture inside the frame on the end table. The murdered Lakota girl with dark mournful snowdrifts for eyes. The cold is too cold. Snow keeps rattling the windows. The wood-burning stove burns hot only for a few minutes. Like its smoke could curl down our throats and choke us, yet leave us ice-covered. My body shakes; the thin blankets aren't warm enough. He sits on the floor wrapped in a blanket with his back against the couch. I could touch his hair. Outside is the frozen world without leaves; the trees creak like attic stairs. Outside Godzilla fights the Snow Behemoth.

He hunches his shoulders and makes a pallet on the floor. "Are you cold, Jana? I like that name better than 77."

"Please, I'm freezing." I ask him to lie next to me on the couch I'm so cold. Please. Will it hurt for him to put his arms around me? I turn my back to him and he fits himself against me. He takes me in his arms. We lie against each other fully clothed holding the other's body heat close. Later, I'll remember dreaming of snow and Mr. Sells and the snow hitting like tiny hammers. I'll shake in Wiley's arms as Mr. Sells has me sit; he'll sense my whole body trembling and my fingers looking for a handrailing, a wall, anything. He wants to call a doctor. No doctor. No doctor. I'll be all right. I slip off my flats and wiggle my foot into my tap shoes. Wiley breathes on the back of my neck, buries his nose in my hair. I'm a cold pane of glass iced over and where he breathes the ice melts. The snow is angry and I like it howling.

"If we take our clothes off we'll be warmer," I stammer, rolling over to face him. He pushes the hair out of my eyes, brushes my cheek with his knuckles, and tells me it's not a good idea. I'm a kid and he's a man. "I am expected to live only six more years," I say with a catch in my throat. "I heard the doctor tell that to my mom. They're my six years and I'll never do anything again I don't want to. But I want good things to happen too." I want him to kiss me, more than I want to wake up in the morning. More than I want to walk again. I breathe in his skin's smell of sagebrush. Won't you take me far away from the world?

"Sleep, Jana. Just sleep. I don't want you to come to harm."

"But I'm already harmed." I think of his fiancée's killer, Joe Hawk, his footsteps in the snow. The bringer of harm. Then, miraculously, his footsteps shuffle away. I listen, following them into the snow, the footsteps dragging something. The Big Dipper is spilling tiny drops of snow onto me, tickling my belly.

"You just don't want to kiss me because I'm a gimp," I accuse. Then I feel his lips on mine. Like a place you're ready to be stranded forever.

When he stops kissing me, he strokes my hair. "I think you're beautiful. But you're too young. Now go to sleep."

South Dakota, the law says the age of consent is 16 and that's not exactly my age. When he asked me how old I was I lied. I'm fifteen going on sixteen.

※ ※ ※

I'll know later what I don't know now. I'll wake up, the wind still blowing, the twilight of day without sun, a day of eclipse. Wiley's not beside me. He's out in the storm cutting wood. I'll need to pee, to wash, I'll need to eat. He's pushed my wheelchair against the couch. I'll roll into the kitchen, reach up and open one of the cupboards. I'll pull the silverware drawer and use a wooden spatula to push down some noodles. Finding a spoon of butter, I'll fry the butter and mix in the noodles. Lots of pepper, it'll be good. The package cost 65 cents. I'll wheel into the bathroom. One of those old tubs with black-pink tile. I'll turn on the taps and wash my face with the last of the cold water in the pipes. I'll brush my hair with Wiley's brush and imagine JadeDragon's green horse with a long mane of cornsilk, a braid of green from her chin, her neck longer than a horse's but shorter than a giraffe's. It will be hard to turn around in the bathroom. Yet I won't want to leave ever. Wiley calls my name. Jana. I'll roll toward him, toward my name. He's at the door. His arms full. He needs me to open it. The knob takes a long time to turn, but I get it open. He carries in an armload of wood; wood chips settle in his loose hair that falls over his shoulder. Maybe I'll say, "My clothes are dirty. Can I wear some of yours?" He'll try the noodle gunk. "This tastes good. So you can cook." He points to an upright closet. It latches with brass. I choose a silk shirt, white and brown like a leopard only striped. I ask if he has any jeans. Of course he does, except he's 6 feet tall, and I'm 5 feet two. But that doesn't count anymore, because he'll never see me standing up. This is perfect, a blizzard, snowed in. I'll think of it always as Godzilla's blizzard.

* * *

After two days, a pure white morning appears. Silence. Everywhere drifts of snow and Wiley's gingerbread house half-buried. A grove of pines and oaks. A little brown driveway. I'll see the house in daylight. A pale tangerine. I'll recognize the police when they show up. The very policeman who bought coffee a million years ago in Dunkin' Donuts. The one with a doorknob for a head. The cruiser's red police bubble will bleed into the snow. They'll come to arrest Wiley. For kidnapping. You likely escaped a bad fate, the wind will say. Look what happened to Liliane. You're crazy, I'll curse the wind. I'll see Wiley in handcuffs.

I'll fight to free him. I'll swear leaving Crippled Children's was all my idea. Godzilla with the help of JadeDragon_77 will get the charges dropped. But I'll never see Wiley again.

JadeDragon's theme song likes to play in my sleep, a music that is almost beyond hearing from a sound track found in Destoroyah. It's a song that sounds like the sun and moon are shining at the same time or a watery melody that guitarfish thrum.

KATHRYN NUERNBERGER

The Symbolical Head *(1883)* as *When Was the Last Time?*

What faculties, when perverted, most degrade the mind?
What faculties, when perverted, does it cost most to gratify?
I undertook to discover the soul in the body—
I looked in the pineal gland, I looked
in the vena cava. I looked in every
perforating arterial branch. With the fingers
of my right, I touched the Will and the Ring
of Solomon on the left. For a second
I felt sprung. Then bereft as ever.
Someone used to love me. Someone
used to see me. If you open a person up,
purple, pulsing. It's in here somewhere, scalpel,
and in and in. Let's walk in the woods,
as we once did, and see if we can find a snail,
its shell covered in symbiotic lichen.
When you covered my lichen in yours,
I thought that's what we wanted—
to be rock and moss and slug and all of it.
To be simultaneously thinking of snails,
which are so beautifully stony
and marvelously squished.
Wasn't that what we wanted?
I went to your lecture. I thought it
best to retrace my steps. You were trying
to explain—*If I were to put my fingers directly on your brain…*
I wish you would, how I wish you would
trace the seagull diving towards the water
as a whale rises up, the anchor dropped, the gray
linen slacks, all the polygons of my this and that
jigsawing under your touch. Oh yes, let's
do that. Let's vivisect my brain and see
if it's in there. You have your porcelain man
with the black-lined map of his longing.
You have your pointer and your glasses
and your pen. I hear you ask the class, *What faculties,*
having ascendancy, are deaf to reason? What faculty,
when large, brightens every object on which we look?
I miss you, you know. I miss you so.

Or Perhaps Not

The gnome lived in the gold fields
of the princess's hair. She brushed him
and hail fell on his thatched roof,
but still she never knew he was there,
lighting his small fires in the glen
of her curls, roasting pumpkin seeds
and spitting the husks into the hay.

Did he know there was a princess?
Did he know the cruel king
she was made to marry threw her
roughly to the bed as she cried into a pillow?
Did he know when her firstborn son
was lost in a bloody sluice?

It's hard to say what he knew,
since it may be God is a deceiver
and it may be that we deceive ourselves,
and also who can say
whether gnomes are real and what
they know of loneliness
in the midst of their perfect solitude.

What can be said is night fell
on the gnome lying among
the thorn-clutched wheatberry
and rosy bramble of her braids
as he watched, or perhaps did not,
the revolutions of ram, rabbit, maiden,
and hydra, the sun against his back
going gray, as he stuffed fresh tobacco
in his pipe and puffed smoke rings
around the stars they held in common.

René Descartes and the Clockwork Girl

In man, it was written, *are found the elements*
and their characteristics, for he passes
from cold to hot, moisture to dryness.
He comes into being and passes out of being
like the minerals, nourishes and reproduces
like the plants, has feeling and life
like animals. His figure resembles the terebinth;
his hair, grass; veins, arteries; rivers, canals;
and his bones, the mountains.

Then the vascular system was discovered.
Pump and pulley replaced wind and mill
sweeping blood down those dusty roads.
And Descartes, the first to admit
he supposed a body to be nothing
but a machine made of earth. Mere clockwork.
He found this a comfort, because
you can always wind a machine back up.

The *Chimera* was a clock in the form of a leviathan,
Memento Mori was the shape of skull.
Spheres and pendants, water droplets and pears.
Milkmaids tugging udders on the hour.
Some kept time using Berthold's new equation,
some invented the second hand. The *Silver Swan*
sits in a stream of glass ripples and gilded leaves,
swallowing silver-plated fish as music plays.

After Descartes's daughter died,
he took to the sea. They say he went
so mad with grief he remade her
as automaton. A wind-up cog and lever
elegy hidden in the cargo hold.

He said the body is a machine
and he may well be right about that.
But when she was so hot with fever

she could not breathe, and then so suddenly cold,
he held his fingers on her wrist and felt
only his own heart pumping. All the wind
and water of a daughter became a vast meadow
that has no design and no function
and there is no way beyond that stretch of grass.

Grief, the sailors said, is a hex
and contagion and it will draw the wind
down from the sails. It will stopper
in the glass jar sitting like a heart
in the chamber of a mechanical girl
with mechanical glass eyes. On a ship beleaguered
by storm, they ripped open the box
with a crowbar to find the automaton
Descartes called *Francine* because he missed
saying her name. They threw her into the wake
and his face became a moon in the black
deep, each wave lapping it under.

He supposed that if you thought hard enough
you should be able to understand,
for example, how a stick would refract
in water even if you had never seen a stick
or water or the light of day. By this means,
he said, your mind will be delivered.

If you think hard enough, you can light a fire
in the hearth. Your child can press herself
against your knee and snug her shoulder into yours
as you wind the clock of a girl like and unlike her,
who can walk three remarkable skips and blink
and curtsy politely before ticking down.

It may be there is no wind blowing
blood through the body, but, arm around her,
you feel how she flushes with fiery amazement
as she puts her little hand over her own
cuckooing heart, because this is what we do
when papa has taken our breath away.

ED FRANKEL

Among Other Things, Joyce Said

Ulysses was about "ineluctable certitude
and the affirmation of the void."
The one word everyone knows
speaks for itself, and facts, like the body,
that hermetic organ, sealed in its own warm juices,
take on a beauty of their own.
The Big Yes and The Big No
ply their oily questions and answers,
push and pull, until tendon answers tendon
and bone answers bone.

Even the Gods couldn't change Fate.
Zeus wept at the death of Sarpedon,
his half-human son, consoled, if Gods are consoled,
by whatever engendered the fire that turns
bone wrapped in fat to smoldering ash.

Lots of certainty for Homer who knew
his listeners would reach for their spears
when the suitors abused Penelope.
Paris, the pouter pigeon, swelled up
with the truth of his member,
the courage and morality of a gland.
Helen, in the end, murmured her regrets,
which is more than most of them did.

Blazes Boylan, another puffed-up pigeon.
Molly has her doubts about him
when he pats her behind like the rump
of a racehorse he is certain will win,
before the dark horse makes it home.
She loves him, she loves him not.
What *is* "the word everyone knows"?

Sooner or later, we all deal with The Big No,
which also speaks for itself from across the abyss,
assumes the position, neck outstretched,
hisses like a goose, and eats its own children.

Ed Frankel

The rest is all hearsay and second-hand experience,
what we hear on the street or read in the *Freeman's Journal*
that Bloom sold ads for and carried under his arm.

Young Stephan Daedalus, wet and green,
the imperfect prince of a bankrupt king
sets out on the same waters
we all cross, behind our special oar,
not yet lying with our gear on our chest
slathered in pitch and oil, soon to light up
the "limb loosening" darkness.

Or is it as simple as that kidney, in the beginning of *Ulysses*,
a bit overcooked, sealed in its juices,
left frying in the pan?

As simple as whatever is exchanged between us at this moment,
mute as the currents of the ocean
or this hermetic vessel, sleek-hulled enough
to ride out the storm, or wait out the doldrums
while we find our seat at the rowing bench,
dip in the oars and pull, pull
till we get the thing moving again.
Until the right wind comes up
to take us out to the open sea
where we look to Orion and the Pole Star
to guide us home, to Ithaca
or that narrow house on Eccles Street

where we lie head to foot in our feathery bed,
navigate the swells, and doubts,
beneath the scented sheets.
The musk-blown Yes fills the room
in blowsy clouds of memory,
in long perfumey breaths that shut our eyes
which is not the darkness of "limb loosening death."
And we listen to the warm sap run
in the living tree of our marriage bed.

Mark Weiss, photograph

About the Authors

EDWARD ADAMS lives and works in Baltimore, a fine place for a writer because the city demands you stay alert, look around, pay attention. New work by Adams has been published or is forthcoming in *Harpur Palate, Green Hills Literary Lantern,* and *Confrontation.*

SUZE BARON is Hatian-American. She is a registered nurse and a family tree enthusiast.

E. LOUISE BEACH is a poet, critic, translator, and librettist. She has set eight poem cycles and the libretti for two operas. *Ophelia's Flowers* was performed this March at the Women in Music Festival at the Eastman School of Music. Beach's *Elegy* was given at Pennsylvania's Dickinson College in May, 2011.

EMILY BENSON received her B.A. from Cornell University and her M.F.A. from Goddard College. She is an adjunct English professor at LaGuardia Community College in Queens, New York, where she teaches poetry and creative writing. She lives in Williamsburg, Brooklyn, with her husband and two adopted stray cats. She recently published a review of J.M. Coetzee's *Summertime* in *Colorado Review*. These are her first published poems.

DENISE BERGMAN is the author of *Seeing Annie Sullivan* (poems about the early life of Helen Keller's teacher) and the editor of the anthology *City River of Voices*. Her poems have been published widely. An excerpt of her poem "Red," about the neighborhood near a slaughterhouse, is permanently installed as public art in Cambridge, Massachusetts.

KARINA BOROWICZ's forthcoming book, *The Bees Are Waiting*, was selected by Franz Wright for the 2011 Marick Press Poetry Prize. Her work has also appeared in *AGNI, Poetry Northwest,* and *The Southern Review.*

BARBARA SWIFT BRAUER is a freelance writer and editor living in San Geronimo, California. Her work has appeared in *West Marin Review, The MacGuffin, Spillway, The Pedestal Magazine,* and *Zone 3*, and in anthologies, including *The Place That Inhabits Us*. She is the author with Jackie Kirk of *Witness: The Artist's Vision in The Face of AIDS*. Her full-length poetry collection is forthcoming from Sixteen Rivers Press.

CATHERINE BROWDER's work has appeared in *Prairie Schooner, Shenandoah, New Letters,* and *Green Mountains Review*. Her most recent collection of stories, *Secret Lives*, was published by Southern Methodist University Press. She is an advisory editor at *New Letters*.

T. ALAN BROUGHTON lives in Burlington, Vermont. A recipient of a Guggenheim Fellowship and an NEA Award, he has published novels, poems and stories. His most recent books are his seventh collection of poems, *A World Remembered* (Carnegie Mellon University Press, 2010), and a book of short stories, *Suicidal Tendencies* (Colorado State University Press, 2003).

RICK BURSKY's book, *Death Obscura*, was released by Sarabande Books in late 2010. Bear Star Press published his earlier book, *The Soup of Something Missing*. His poems have appeared in many journals including *The American Poetry Review*, *The Iowa Review*, *The Southern Review*, *Harvard Review*, *Prairie Schooner*, *Black Warrior Review*, *Shenandoah*, and *New Letters*. Bursky works in advertising and teaches poetry at The University of California Los Angeles Extension.

GRACE CAVALIERI's latest publication is a novella in verse, *Millie's Sunshine Tiki Villas* (Casa Menendez). She now celebrates thirty-five years on-air with "The Poet and the Poem," recorded at the Library of Congress for public radio. Her new play, "Anna Nicole: Blonde Glory," opened in New York City in 2011.

ROBIN CHAPMAN is author of seven books of poetry, most recently *The Eelgrass Meadow* (Tebot Bach). Her poems have appeared recently in *Alaska Quarterly Review*, *Prairie Schooner*, and *Qarrtsiluni*, and in the Milwaukee Public Zoo. She co-edited *Love After 60: an anthology of women's poems* and is recipient of the 2010 Helen Howe Poetry Prize from *Appalachia*.

SUSAN COHEN's first full-length book of poems, *Throat Singing*, is forthcoming in 2012. Her poetry has appeared most recently in *CALYX*, *Poetry East*, *River Styx*, and *Southern Poetry Review*, and in anthologies from Salmon Poetry and City Works Press. She lives in Berkeley, California, and has twice received the National Association of Science Writers Science in Society Award.

JIM DANIELS's most recent books include *Trigger Man* (Michigan State University Press), *Having a Little Talk with Capital P Poetry* (Carnegie Mellon University Press), and *All of the Above* (Adastra Press). He has also written three films, most recently *Mr. Pleasant*. A native of Detroit, Daniels lives in Pittsburgh near the boyhood homes of Dan Marino and Andy Warhol.

STEPHANIE DICKINSON lives in New York City. Her novel, *Half Girl*, was published by Spuyten Duyvil. *Corn Goddess* and *Road of Five Churches* are available from Rain Mountain Press. Her stories are reprinted in *Best American Nonrequired Reading* and *New Stories from the South*. "Between the Cold Hearts and Blue Dudes" was the winner of *New Delta Review's* 2011 Matt Clark Fiction prize.

PATRICIA FARGNOLI has published six collections of poetry. Her newest book, *Then, Something* (Tupelo Press, fall 2009), won the ForeWord Poetry Book of the Year Award Silver Award and the Shelia Mooton Book Award. She's published poems recently in *Harvard Review, Green Mountains Review, Alaska Quarterly Review, Massachusetts Review,* and *Poetry International.* A MacDowell Fellow, she was the New Hampshire Poet Laureate from 2006-2009.

ED FRANKEL is a poet who lives in Los Angeles, California.

MARITA GARIN edited *Southern Appalachian Poetry: An Anthology of Works by 37 Poets* (2008). She has received fellowships from the Tennessee Arts Commission, the North Carolina Arts Council, and MacDowell Colony. Her poems have appeared recently in *Cold Mountain Review, Potomac Review,* and *Connecticut Review.* She lives in Black Mountain, North Carolina, where she writes full time.

ANDREW GRACE's third book of poems, *Sancta*, was recently published by Ahsahta Press. He is a Ph.D. candidate in creative writing at the University of Cincinnati.

JONATHAN GREENHAUSE is the author of a chapbook, *Sebastian's Relativity* (Anobium Books), and his poems have appeared in *The Believer, Fjords, New Delta Review, The South Carolina Review, Water~Stone Review,* and elsewhere. He has received two Pushcart nominations and was a runner-up in the 2012 *Georgetown Review* Prize and a semi-finalist for the 2011 Paumanok Poetry Award.

JEFF GUNDY's most recent books are *Spoken among the Trees* (Akron, 2007), winner of the Society of Midland Authors Poetry Award, and *Deerflies* (WordTech Editions, 2000). His new work is in *The Sun, Image, The Cincinnati Review, Kestrel, Fifth Wednesday Journal,* and *Poetry Salzburg Review.* A 2008 Fulbright lecturer at the University of Salzburg, he teaches at Bluffton University in Ohio.

JEFFERSON HARRIS's poems have appeared in *Exquisite Corpse: A Journal of Letters and Life, RATTLE, The Summerset Review, Pearl, The Gay and Lesbian Review,* and other publications. A former senior editor at the Getty Museum, he lives in Santa Monica, California.

IHAB HASSAN has received two Guggenheim and three Fulbright Fellowships, and two honorary doctorates from the Universities of Uppsala and Giessen. He is the author of fifteen books of essays and memoirs, and of many short stories, published in such journals as *AGNI* and *The Antioch*

About the Authors

Review. He has just completed a novelette and stories with Egyptian backgrounds, *The Changeling and Other Stories*.

DARRELL ALEJANDRO HOLNES's work has appeared in *The Caribbean Writer*, *Minnesota Review*, *Bestiary Magazine*, and other places. He has an M.F.A. from The University of Michigan.

ANN HOSTETLER is the author of a volume of poetry, *Empty Room with Light*, and the editor of *A Cappella: Mennonite Voices in Poetry* (Iowa 2003). Her poems have appeared in *Adanna*, *The American Scholar*, *Cream City Review*, *Literary Mama*, *Poet Lore*, *Porcupine*, *Washington Square*, and other publications. She teaches English and creative writing at Goshen College in Goshen, Indiana, and is editor of the *Journal of the Center for Mennonite Writing*.

BRAD JOHNSON is an associate professor at Palm Beach State College and has two chapbooks, *Void Where Prohibited* and *The Happiness Theory* (puddinghouse.com), and a third chapbook, *Gasoline Rainbow* (finishinglinepress.com). Work of his has recently been accepted by *Jabberwock Review*, *The Madison Review*, *Natural Bridge*, *The South Carolina Review*, *The Southeast Review*, *Steam Ticket*, *Willow Springs*, and other journals.

KITTY JOSPÉ lives in Rochester, New York. After years of teaching French, she has turned to teaching poetry (in English) and linking word to art as a docent at the Memorial Art Gallery. She holds an M.A. in French Literature from New York University and an M.F.A. in Poetry from Pacific University, Oregon, and is working on her second book.

VICTORIA KELLY received her B.A. from Harvard University, her M.F.A. from the Iowa Writers' Workshop, and her M.Phil. in Creative Writing from Trinity College, Dublin. Her poetry has appeared in *Alaska Quarterly Review*, and her fiction has been published in *Colorado Review*, *The Greensboro Review*, and *Fiction Magazine*, among others. She lives in Virginia Beach, Virginia, with her husband, a fighter pilot for the U.S. Navy.

BECKY KENNEDY is a linguist and a college professor who lives in Jamaica Plain, Massachusetts. Her poetry has appeared in many magazines and journals; her work has also been nominated for a Pushcart Prize and has appeared on *Verse Daily*. She has a chapbook forthcoming from Finishing Line Press.

KATHLEEN KIRK is the author of four poetry chapbooks and the poetry editor for *Escape Into Life*. Her work appears in a variety of print and online literary journals, including *Confrontation, LEVELER, Poetry East*, and *Spoon River Poetry Review*. She is a Pushcart Prize nominee and the winner of the 2011 Ekphrasis Prize from *Ekphrasis*.

RACHEL INEZ LANE lives in Washington, D.C. Her work has appeared in the *Orlando Sentinel* and the *Los Angeles Times*. Recently her poetry has appeared in *Washington Square, RATTLE,* and as a finalist in the 2011 Pablo Neruda Prize for Poetry given by *Nimrod*. She holds an M.F.A. in Creative Writing from Florida State University, and is working on her first book of poetry, entitled *This Heart Goes Bang*.

REBECCA LEHMANN is the author of the poetry collection *Between the Crackups*, which won the Salt Crashaw Prize and is forthcoming from Salt Publishing. Her poems have been published in *Tin House, The Gettysburg Review, The Iowa Review,* and other journals. She holds an M.F.A. from the Iowa Writers' Workshop, a Ph.D. from Florida State University, and has been awarded residencies at the Millay Colony for the Arts and the Vermont Studio Center.

BRYCE LILLMARS was born and raised in Danville, Pennsylvania. After graduating from the College-Conservatory of Music at the University of Cincinnati in 2009, he left his bassoon at his parents' house and moved to Oaxaca, Mexico. He has been teaching English and eating tamales ever since. This is his first publication.

DANIEL LUSK is author of *Lake Studies: Meditations on Lake Champlain, Kissing the Ground: New & Selected Poems,* and other books. Besides appearances in *Nimrod*, his poems have been published in *Poetry, New Letters, Prairie Schooner, The Iowa Review, The American Poetry Review, North American Review,* and many other literary journals. In 2006 his poems earned second place in *Nimrod's* Pablo Neruda Poetry Prize competition. He teaches poetry and creative writing at the University of Vermont.

MEKEEL MCBRIDE is the author of six books of poetry, all from Carnegie-Mellon University Press, including *Dog Star Delicatessen (New and Selected Poems 1979-2006)*. She teaches in the undergraduate and M.F.A. programs at the University of New Hampshire and lives in Maine, on the Piscataqua River, where she loves to row in her wooden dory.

JULIANNA MCCARTHY, who lives in the Los Padres National Forest with two cats and a dog, has been a first-prize winner in MDHS's Bridge competition, a Schieble Sonnet Prize winner, a Pushcart Prize nominee, and a Marsh Hawk Press Prize finalist. Her poems have appeared in *The Antioch*

About the Authors

Review, Alehouse, Spot Literary Magazine, Boxcar Poetry Review, Best Poem, Tidal Basin Review, and the *Crow Talk* and *Don't Blame the Ugly Mug* anthologies.

NATHAN MCCLAIN currently lives and works in Los Angeles. His poems have recently appeared or are forthcoming in *Columbia Poetry Review, Cave Wall, Water~Stone Review, DIAGRAM, Pebble Lake Review*, and *Best New Poets 2010*.

SALLY ALLEN MCNALL has published steadily since 1985 in a wide variety of journals and magazines. Her chapbook, *How to Behave at the Zoo and Other Lessons*, won a State Street Press competition in 1997, and her book, *Rescue*, won the Backwaters Press Prize in 1999. Her new book, *Where Once*, was chosen for publication by *Main Street Rag* in 2010.

LATANYA MCQUEEN has been published in *The North American Review, Potomac Review, Fourteen Hills, The Robert Olen Butler Prize Stories, Monkeybicycle*, and *War, Literature and the Arts*, among other publications.

NADINE SABRA MEYER's first book of poems, *The Anatomy Theater*, won the National Poetry Series in 2006. Her poems have won the New Letters Prize for Poetry, the 2011 Meridian Editor's Prize, and a Pushcart Prize. Her poems have appeared or are forthcoming in *The Southern Review, Southwest Review, Ploughshares, Shenandoah Journal, Boulevard, The Missouri Review*, and *Blackbird*. She is an Assistant Professor at Gettysburg College.

TRAVIS MOSSOTTI was awarded the 2011 May Swenson Poetry Award for his first book, *About the Dead* (2011, Utah State University Press), and the 2009 James Hearst Poetry Prize from *The North American Review* for his poem "The Dead Cause." In 2010 his poem, "Decampment," was adapted to the screen as an animated short film.

BENJAMIN MYERS won the Oklahoma Book Award for Poetry for his first book, *Elegy for Trains* (Village Books Press, 2010). His poems have appeared or are forthcoming in *The New York Quarterly, Iron Horse Literary Review, Measure, Plainsongs*, and many other journals. He teaches literature and writing at Oklahoma Baptist University.

JOHN A. NIEVES has poems forthcoming or recently published in such journals as *Indiana Review, Hayden's Ferry Review, The New York Quarterly, Ninth Letter, Valparaiso Poetry Review*, and *The Cincinnati Review*. He won the 2011 *Indiana Review* Poetry Prize and the 2010 *Southeast Review* AWP Short Poetry contest. He is currently a Ph.D. candidate at the University of Missouri.

About the Authors

KATHRYN NUERNBERGER is the author of *Rag & Bone*, which was the winner of Elixir Press's Antivenom Prize. She teaches at the University of Central Missouri, where she also serves as poetry editor of *Pleiades*. Her poems appear in *West Branch*, *Copper Nickel*, and *Burnside Review*.

MARTIN OTT is a former U.S. Army interrogator who currently lives in Los Angeles, and still finds himself asking a lot of questions. His fiction has appeared in more than twenty magazines, including a previous issue of *Nimrod*. His book of poetry, *Captive*, won the De Novo Prize and will be published by C&R Press in 2012. *Poets' Guide to America*—a collaboration with John F. Buckley—will be published by Brooklyn Arts Press in 2012.

ERIC PANKEY is the author of eight collections of poetry, the most recent of which is *The Pear As One Example: New And Selected Poems 1984-2008*. A new collection, *Dissolve*, is forthcoming from Milkweed Editions in 2013. He is the Heritage Chair in Writing in the M.F.A. program at George Mason University.

LINDA PASTAN's thirteenth book of poems, *Traveling Light*, has recently been published by Norton. She was Poet Laureate of Maryland from 1991 to 1995 and has been a finalist twice for the National Book Award. In 2003, she won the Ruth Lilly Poetry Prize.

ANGELA PATTEN is author of two poetry collections, *Reliquaries* and *Still Listening*, both published by Salmon Poetry, Ireland. Her poems have appeared in several anthologies and in numerous literary journals. She teaches poetry and creative writing at the University of Vermont. A native of Dublin, Ireland, she now lives in Burlington, Vermont, with her husband, poet Daniel Lusk.

THOMAS PATTERSON's work has appeared in *The South Carolina Review*, *Chiron Review*, *Nimrod*, *The Cider Press Review*, and *Cavalier Literary Couture*, and he has work forthcoming in *The Louisville Review*.

ELEANOR PAYNTER has roots in Texas and Rome and holds an M.F.A. from Sarah Lawrence College. Her work has recently appeared or is forthcoming in *elimae*, *The Innisfree Poetry Journal*, *New Madrid*, *Salamander*, and *THRUSH*. Two of her poems were awarded honorable mention in the 2011 Winning Writers War Poetry Contest. She lives in the Netherlands.

GAIL PECK is the author of two full-length collections of poetry and three chapbooks, most recently *From Terezin*. Her poems and essays have been published in numerous journals including *The Southern Review*, *The Greens-*

About the Authors

boro Review, *Nimrod*, *Cimarron Review*, *Mississippi Review*, *Rattle*, *Cave Wall*, and *Brevity*, and her work has been widely anthologized. Her collection *Counting the Lost* is forthcoming this fall from *Main Street Rag*.

SIMON PERCHIK is an attorney whose poems have appeared in *Partisan Review*, *The New Yorker*, and elsewhere.

MARGE PIERCY has published 18 poetry collections including *What Are Big Girls Made Of?*, *The Crooked Inheritance*, and, this year, *Hunger Moon: New and Selected Poems 1980—2011*, all from Knopf. She has written seventeen novels, most recently, *Sex Wars*, and a memoir, *Sleeping with Cats*. PM Press is republishing her novel *Vida* this December.

INES P. RIVERA PROSDOCIMI received her M.F.A. in Creative Writing from American University. Her work has appeared in the *Afro-Hispanic Review*, *Bellevue Literary Review*, *Alaska Quarterly Review*, *Cold Mountain Review*, *International Poetry Review*, *Poet Lore*, *Puerto del Sol*, *The Caribbean Writer*, *Wasafiri*, *Witness*, *Yellow Medicine Review*, and elsewhere. She teaches at Northern Virginia Community College.

DIAN DUCHIN REED is the author of *Medusa Discovers Styling Gel* (Finishing Line Press, 2009). Recent poems appear in *Prairie Schooner*, *Poet Lore*, and *Poetry East*. She has been the recipient of a Sundberg Family grant for literary criticism, the Mel Tuohey Award for writing excellence, and the Mary Lonnberg Smith Award in Poetry.

CHRISTOPHER ROBINSON is a writer, teacher, and translator. He earned his M.A. in poetry from Boston University and his M.F.A. from Hunter College. His work has appeared in *Alaska Quarterly Review*, *Night Train*, *Kenyon Review*, *Umbrella Factory*, *McSweeney's*, and elsewhere. He is a recipient of fellowships from the MacDowell Colony and the Virginia Center for the Creative Arts.

GERI ROSENZWEIG was born in Ireland and worked there as an R.N. Her work has appeared in such journals as *Hotel Amerika*, *Rattle*, *Borderlands: Texas Poetry Review*, and *Cave Wall*. She has published one collection of poems and two chapbooks; a new book of poems is "out there." Her work has won the BBC Poet of the Year award, the Walt Whitman Society of Long Island Award, and has appeared in many anthologies.

JAMIE ROSS paints and writes on a mesa west of Taos, New Mexico. His poetry has appeared in many journals, including *Poetry East*, *Nimrod*, *The Texas Review*, *Northwest Review*, and *The Paris Review*, and the anthology *Best*

New Poets 2007. His collection, *Vinland*, was awarded the 2008 Intro Prize from Four Way Books.

Lee Rossi's latest book is *Wheelchair Samurai*. His poems, reviews, and interviews have appeared in *Harvard Review*, *The Sun*, *Poetry Northwest*, *Chelsea*, *Beloit Poetry Journal*, and *Southern Poetry Review*. He is a staff reviewer and interviewer for the online magazine *Pedestal*. He lives in the San Francisco Bay Area.

Margaret Rozga is the author of two books of poetry. Her first book, *Two Hundred Nights and One Day*, won a bronze medal in poetry in the 2009 Independent Publishers Book Awards and was named an outstanding achievement for 2009 by the Wisconsin Library Association. Her new book, *Though I Haven't Been to Baghdad*, includes two poems originally published in *Nimrod*.

Tomaž Šalamun lives in Ljubljana, Slovenia. He taught Spring semester 2011 at Michener Center for Writers at The University of Texas. His recent books translated into English are *Woods and Chalices* (Harcourt 2008), *Poker* (Ugly Duckling Presse, second edition 2008), *There's the Hand and There's the Arid Chair* (Counterpath Press, 2009) and *The Blue Tower* (Houghton Mifflin Harcourt, 2011).

Lisa D. Schmidt lives south of Seattle, Washington, where she works as an orchestra teacher and violist. More poems of hers can be found in recent issues of *Avocet*, *Windfall*, *The Evansville Review*, and *The Bitter Oleander Press*, as well as in forthcoming issues of *Quarterly West* and *Ann Arbor Review*.

Penelope Scambly Schott's books include a lyric collection, *May the Generations Die in the Right Order*, and a verse biography, *A is for Anne: Mistress Hutchinson Disturbs the Commonwealth*. She was a semi-finalist for *Nimrod*'s 2008 and 2011 Pablo Neruda Prize for Poetry. She lives in Portland, Oregon.

Matt Schumacher has published two collections of poetry, *Spilling the Moon* and *The Fire Diaries*. His poems have recently appeared in *Fourteen Hills* and *Green Mountains Review*. Poetry editor of *Phantom Drift*, a journal of New Fabulism, he recently completed a Ph.D. in English, as well as a book of fantastical drinking songs. He lives in Rhododendron, Oregon.

Vince Sgambati retired early to dedicate his time to parenting and writing, after teaching for thirty years. He has written an online column

About the Authors

about gay parenting called *Vince's View*; most of these personal essays have appeared nationally in LGBT magazines. His work has been published in the anthology *Queer and Catholic* (Routledge) and the *Journal of GLBT Family Studies*. He lives in Central New York with his partner of thirty-five years, their fifteen-year-old son, and two dogs.

CLARK SMITH is a poet who lives in Colorado Springs, Colorado.

MYRA SHAPIRO's poems have appeared in many periodicals and anthologies including *The Best American Poetry* 1999 and 2003. She serves on the board of directors of Poets House and teaches poetry workshops for the International Women's Writing Guild. Her book of poems, *I'll See You Thursday*, was published by Blue Sofa Press in 1999, and in 2007 Chicory Blue Press published her memoir, *Four Sublets: Becoming a Poet in New York*.

LEROY N. SORENSON has been writing since he was a teenager: essays, commentary, short stories, and poetry. His day jobs have included child psychologist, political organizer, and financial analyst. In 2009-2010, he was one of four poets selected for the Loft Literary Center Mentor Series. He lives with his wife in St. Paul, Minnesota, but writes poetry in Mexico each January.

CHRISTINE HOPE STARR's poetry and essays have appeared or are forthcoming in *Cider Press Review, Compass Rose, Confrontation, Eclipse, Permafrost, Soundings East, Spoon River Poetry Review, Studio One, Whiskey Island*, and elsewhere. She holds an M.F.A. from Vermont College of Fine Arts, which nominated her for Best New Poets 2009. She teaches writing (and vigorous inquiry) at Doane College in Nebraska.

JOHN SUROWIECKI, a former Pablo Neruda Prize winner, is the author of three books of poetry as well as five chapbooks. A sixth chapbook, *Mr. Z., Mrs. Z., J.Z., S.Z.*, has been recently published by Ugly Duckling Presse. His poems also appear in *The Hecht Prize Anthology* (Waywiser Press) and *The Sunken Garden Anthology* (Wesleyan Press).

MICHAEL THOMAS TAREN's poems have appeared in *Colorado Review, Poetikon*, and *Fence*. His chapbook *08 September 2009* was published by Factory Hollow Press. His translations of Tomaž Šalamun have been published by *A Public Space, Poetry Review* (UK), *Fence, Jubilat, LIT, Poetry London*, and elsewhere. His book *Puberty* was a 2009 finalist for the *Fence* Poetry Series, and his book *Motherhood* was a 2010 finalist. He spent nine months (2010—2011) in Slovenia on Fulbright.

JANE VINCENT TAYLOR lives in Oklahoma City. Her latest book of poems, *The Lady Victory*, comes out soon from Turning Point. Her previous chapbook, *What Can Be Saved*, will be dramatized in April, 2012, at Michigan State University, Residential College of Arts and Humanities. She teaches writing at Ghost Ranch in Abiquiu, New Mexico.

TARA TAYLOR's poetry has appeared in *Poet Lore*, *Spoon River Poetry Review*, *The Grove Review*, *Inkwell Journal*, and *Merge Poetry*. She holds an M.F.A. in Poetry from North Carolina State University, where she was awarded the 2010 Brenda Smart Poetry Prize.

MOLLY TENENBAUM is the author of *Now* (Bear Star Press, 2007) and *By a Thread* (Van West & Co, 2000). Her honors include a Hedgebrook residency and a 2009 Washington State Artist Trust Fellowship. She plays Appalachian music; her CDs are *Instead of a Pony* and *Goose & Gander*. She teaches music at home and English at North Seattle Community College.

DWAYNE THORPE was brought up in Dodge City, in western Kansas. One of the founding editors of *Tri-Quarterly*, he has continued to publish poems in a wide variety of magazines — most recently in *Prairie Schooner*, *Beloit Poetry Journal*, *Chautauqua*, and *Blue Unicorn*. His first collection, *Finding Pigeon Creek*, was published by Monongahela Press.

FRANCINE MARIE TOLF is the author of *Rain, Lilies, Luck*, a full-length collection of poetry, and *Joliet Girl*, a memoir, both from North Star Press of St. Cloud (2010). Her work has appeared in numerous journals. She has received grants from the Minnesota State Arts Board, the Barbara Deming Foundation, the Loft Literary Center, and the Elizabeth George Foundation.

JOSE TREJO-MAYA is a poet who lives in La Puente, California.

AMY VANIOTIS is a freelance writer and editor living in Portland, Oregon.

MONICA WENDEL is the author of the chapbook *Call it a Window*, forthcoming from Midwest Writing Center Press. She received her M.F.A. in Creative Writing from New York University, and her B.A. in Philosophy from the State University of New York at Geneseo. She teaches English at St. Thomas Aquinas College and lives in Brooklyn.

LAURELYN WHITT's poems have appeared in various journals in Canada and the United States, including *The Malahat Review*, *PRISM international*, *The Fiddlehead*, *Tampa Review*, *Puerto del Sol* and *RATTLE*. Her recent book, *Interstices* (Logan House Press), won the Holland Prize. She lives in Minnedosa, Manitoba, and is a Professor of Native Studies at Brandon University.

WILLIAM WINFIELD WRIGHT is a Fulbright Scholar and a Fishtrap Fellow, was born in California, and lives in Grand Junction, Colorado, where he teaches at Colorado Mesa University. He has published in *Beloit Poetry Journal, Borderlands: Texas Poetry Review, FIELD, Ninth Letter, The Seattle Review, The South Carolina Review, Third Coast,* and elsewhere.

GLENN HERBERT DAVIS was the recipient of a Oklahoma Visual Arts Fellowship in 2006. His work has been exhibited and published nationally. His solo work, "image of one," was exhibited at Berry College.

JAMES K. ZIMMERMAN is the winner of the 2009 Daniel Varoujan Award and the 2009 and 2010 Hart Crane Memorial Poetry Awards. His work appears or is forthcoming in *anderbo.com, Bellingham Review, Rosebud, Inkwell Journal, Hawai'i Pacific Review,* and *Vallum,* among others. He is also a clinical psychologist in private practice and was a singer/songwriter in a previous life.

STAN ZUMBIEL taught English for thirty-five years and has had a hand in raising four children. He first tried to turn his thoughts into poetry in 1967 while serving in the Navy. In January 2008, he received his M.F.A. in Writing from Vermont College of Fine Arts.

About the Artists

DARREN DIRKSEN is an artist living in Locus Grove, Oklahoma. He is represented in Tulsa by Joseph Gierek Fine Art.

LESLIE RINGOLD is a public defender, poet, and photographer. She lives, works, and plays in Venice, California.

JAMES ANDREW SMITH attended the Kansas City Art Institute. He worked for ten years as a designer before formally beginning his art career in 2001. His work is exhibited in Tulsa through Joseph Gierek Gallery.

JOYCE SMITH, a photographer and musician, works as an academic advisor at The University of Tulsa's Henry Kendall College of Arts and Sciences.

ROI J. TAMKIN is an Atlanta-based photographer and writer. His photographs have appeared in *New Letters*, *Folio*, and *Nexus*. He contributes articles and photographs to *Skipping Stones Magazine*. He also exhibits his work locally through galleries and alternative spaces.

DANIEL K. TENNANT received the "Outstanding Airbrush Teacher of the Year Award" by *American Artist Magazine* in 1994. In 2003 he was an honorable mention winner in *The Artist's Magazine* international art competition. Tennant's work has appeared in magazine articles in *American Artist Magazine*, *Watercolor Magazine*, *American Arts Quarterly*, *World Magazine*, and *Airbrush Magazine*, and has been exhibited across the nation. He is the author of the book *Realistic Painting*. He is represented in Tulsa by M A. Doran Gallery.

MARK WEISS, an ophthalmologist in Tulsa, Oklahoma, is an award-winning photographer.

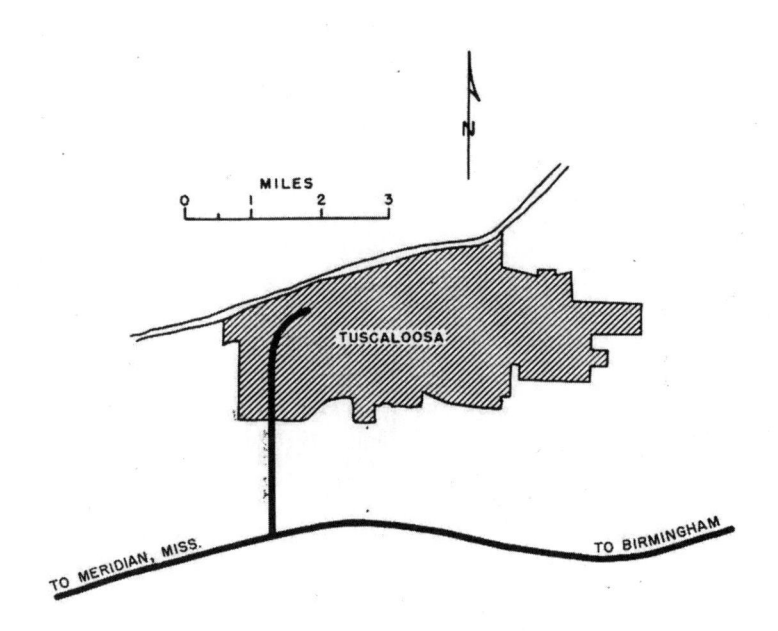

BLACK WARRIOR REVIEW

A preeminent literary journal founded in 1974 at the University of Alabama, *Black Warrior Review* publishes contemporary fiction, poetry, nonfiction, comics, and art by Pulitzer Prize and National Book Award winners alongsides work by new and emerging voices, in addition to a featured poetry chapbook solicited by the editors.

Please visit BWR.UA.EDU for more information, samples of published work, and web-exclusive content.

NORTH AMERICAN
REVIEW

Established in 1815, The North American Review is the oldest literary magazine in the United States and among the oldest in the world. Located at The University of Northern Iowa, The North American Review has published renowned artists and writers such as Rita Dove, Mark Twain, Maxine Hong Kingston, and Walt Whitman. To enjoy our collection of fine poetry, art, fiction, and nonfiction literature subscribe for $22/year or $6.95/copy (US). Visit our online store at www.NorthAmericanReview.org